Frequency of the Dead

by

Jonas Saul

PUBLISHED BY:
Imagine Press Inc.
Ebook ISBN: 978-1-927404-64-5
Paperback ISBN: 978-1-998047-84-0
Hardcover ISBN: 978-1-998047-83-3

The Sarah Roberts Series

Dark Visions (One)
The Warning (Two)
The Crypt (Three)
The Hostage (Four)
The Victim (Five)
The Enigma (Six)
The Vigilante (Seven)
The Rogue (Eight)
Killing Sarah (Nine)
The Antagonist (Ten)
The Redeemed (Eleven)
The Haunted (Twelve)
The Unlucky (Thirteen)
The Abandoned (Fourteen)
The Cartel (Fifteen)
Losing Sarah (Sixteen)
The Pact (Seventeen)
The Terror (Eighteen)
The Chase (Nineteen)
The Betrayal (Twenty)
Sarah's Return (Twenty-One)
The Hunt (Twenty-Two)
The Delivery (Twenty-Three)
The Trap (Twenty-Four)
The Ultimatum (Twenty-Five)
The Depraved (Twenty-Six)
The Condemned (Twenty-Seven)
Payback (Twenty-Eight)
The Unknown (Twenty-Nine)
Wrath (Thirty)
The Damned (Thirty-One)

The Game (Thirty-Two)
The Decoy (Thirty-Three)
The Disappearance (Thirty-Four)
The Whole Truth (Thirty-Five)
Alex (Thirty-Six)
Parkman (Thirty-Seven)
Darwin (Thirty-Eight)
Aaron (Thirty-Nine)
Remains To Be Seen (Forty)

The Jake Wood Novels

The Immortal Gene (Book One)
The Immortal Target (Book Two)

Standalone Novels

What We Were Hiding
The Drowning
The Woman in the Woods
The Threat
The Specter
The Mafia Trilogy
A Murder in Time
Frequency of the Dead

Co-Authored Novels

Collision Course (Written with Gary Ponzo)
There Will Be Blood (Written with Rania Stone)
The Soulless (Written with Rania Stone)
Who I Never Was (Written with Rania Stone)

Short Story Collections

Twisted Fate (Tales of Horror)
Twists of Fate (Tales of Hope)

Chapter 1

WHO KNEW THE DEAD WOULD MAKE her money, pay her rent, and feed her? Since she made a living off the dead, what did that make her? The Grim Reaper wasn't her business partner; that much was true. The fact that her customers were dead had nothing to do with her—it wasn't her fault they'd died. She just talked to them, learned their secrets, and discovered why they were earthbound. After all, she had rent to pay.

Kramer Kay slid her curtains together to cover the kitchen window, blocking the morning sun. The Watersons had requested a morning reading. She abhorred doing readings in the morning but was willing to do it for an additional charge.

Was she proud? Yes. Cheap? No. Could she be bought? Of course. Money talks, and others walk.

Seven separate incense sticks were scattered around the reading room—her kitchen—spewing their odorous smoke. After lighting them in preparation for the reading, Kramer lit two candles on the kitchen table to push back the darkness now that the sunblock curtains were drawn.

Normally, the darkness didn't scare her, but someone on the other side had been pushing through to her for the past few readings, getting stronger—someone unrelated to the individual reading. This entity yearned to be heard in a demanding way.

During her last session two nights ago, the powerful voice swept into the reading and showed Kramer an image of a greater part of downtown Los Angeles destroyed. Darkness had fallen over her soul as the entity said that this devastation was weeks away and that Kramer wouldn't be able to avoid it. The entity had already seen the future, too, and the device that caused the destruction would ignite regardless of what she did.

That was a foolish notion, though. If Kramer was shown a future event, she always had options to stop it. Why would she be shown the event in the first place if it was just meant to tease or taunt her?

Kramer's stomach acted skittish, as if something bad would interrupt this reading, too. Half the time, her readings went pretty well. The other half often involved a skeptical client who taunted her with false details to trip her up. There were sessions where she caught it, but then there were times when she didn't, and the paying customer would demand their money back as she was pronounced a fraud with absolute certainty. Two years ago, she even had a customer call the cops on her, claiming she stole their money under false pretenses.

Today seemed like easy reading, though. There was no

reason for her stomach to be queasy, yet it remained so.

The clock on the wall said she had five minutes left.

She lowered her head and spoke softly to her guide.

"Alweane, stay true to the course and protect us from dark spirits today. Only allow through the two young daughters of this couple who are coming to hear from them. Thank you."

Kramer raised her head and finished the final preparations. She put the kettle on to brew some tea and then sat at the table. Palms facing up, she closed her eyes and felt the room. Energy passed close by. Numerous forces from the other side were present. Her guide's job was to keep them from her lest she lose her mind. Two distinct entities were close, with a third in the background.

A strong, powerful third entity that she felt in her being. She spoke with her mind, asking this powerful entity to remain in the peripheral or leave her presence. There was no one here for them to talk to, nor anyone to listen to them. She urged them mentally to move on and let their issues go.

She felt the entity gazing at her. The force collected itself and rushed toward her. Kramer jolted in her chair as if someone swung to smack her face.

Loud knocking brought her back to the here and now.

Her clients had arrived.

Kramer stood on shaky legs, made the sign of the cross, and kissed the rosary around her neck. As she made her way to the front door, she silently asked Alweane to keep them safe and uninterrupted. She wanted her to force that third entity away and let this reading go as planned.

She opened the door to an older, sad-looking couple a

moment later. The woman appeared worn and weathered with age. The man was old, too, but strong, standing firm with a cold stare.

"Come in, come in. The Watersons, I presume?"

The woman ambled forward as her husband nodded at Kramer. She shut the door behind them, looked to her ceiling, and wondered why she chose this as a career. All her high school planning for her future was for naught.

After being directed to the kitchen, the Watersons sat at the table, getting comfortable without a word. Before she joined them, she lifted the kettle off the stove and set it on a hot plate.

"Would either of you like some tea? Freshly brewed."

Mr. Waterson shook his head in the negative.

So, they wanted to be like that. Okay, I can be all business, too.

Kramer left the kettle on the counter without making a tea and joined them at the table. One of the seven incense sticks was blowing into Mr. Waterson's face. For a moment, Kramer ignored it. Let him be uncomfortable. Social skills were something he seemed to be lacking today.

A moment later, she thought better of it. They were a paying customer, and how they decided to have their visit conducted was apparently going to be on their terms. She had to do what she could to not let them leave her home disjointed.

She reached back to the counter and eased the incense farther away.

Mr. Waterson cleared his throat. "Will you clarify what you are going to do today?" His voice relayed two things to her. One, he didn't like her. And two, he didn't believe in this shit.

Wasn't he in for a show.

"You booked your appointment two days ago—"

"I'm quite aware of when we booked our appointment," Mr. Waterson cut in, his voice hard like a drill sergeant. "Now, I'll ask you again: will you please clarify what you will do here today?"

Kramer took a second to compose herself. If the negativity coming from Mr. Waterson was too powerful, it could alter their experience. It could change the dynamic for the entities coming through, too. Often, people like this controlled and belittled their kin, offering no reason or desire for them to have a visit after they've passed away. Kramer needed to regain control and maintain it for the session if there was any hope of success.

"As I was saying before I was interrupted, when you booked your appointment, I used your names to start an association process with my guide on the other side. My guide acts as a buffer. She locates the ones needed to have a reading and allows them access to me." She stopped and waited, the pause allowing either of them a chance to speak. Neither did, so she continued. "All you need to do is answer my questions as best you can, and I will attempt to answer yours as you voice them. Now, do you have any more questions before we start?"

Mr. Waterson just sat there and glared at her. Mrs. Waterson looked up and slowly shook her head. In those eyes, Kramer saw something like a deep depression, one built over years of wrong choices and the consequences of those choices.

She laid her hands palms up on the table and gestured for the Watersons to join her by clasping her hands, making a unified circle.

Mr. Waterson grunted. "Your hands are cold, clammy, and shaking. Why's that? Nervous about something, Ms. Kay?"

His arrogance didn't faze Kramer. As soon as they started, she would turn Mr. Waterson into a believer, even though he was working hard to keep her from doing her job.

Maybe he was afraid of something. Perhaps his hesitation in belief had more to do with fear and less to do with skepticism.

She would explore that if and when she got the chance. For now, she tilted back her head, closed her eyes, and focused on the entities in the room, ignoring his question. It was time to take control of the session instead of defending herself by battling the customer in a debate of wits.

Kramer felt a female presence nearby and was informed that Waterson's daughters had come through. Kramer detected their movements around the table as well as Alweane's movements.

"I have them here," Kramer whispered. "I will start by telling you that they're happy. They love the other side, our real home. Coming to our plane is a sort of death, but leaving our earthly body is being born again in our true home." She paused, cocking her head slightly to the side, eyes still closed, thankful Mr. Waterson hadn't interrupted her or withdrawn his hand. "They are speaking now. Give me a second to hear them, and I will tell you what they're saying."

Kramer listened with her mind, taking in the conscious thoughts, the images being offered her. While doing so, a part of her was drawn back to the hand Mr. Waterson was grasping as it had grown tense. She pictured him staring at her, his eyes boring into her head. *If looks could kill ...*

The entities in the room drew her back to them.

"I'm hearing …" she began, then added, "Wait, your daughters were twins. I can see that now." Kramer opened her eyes and glanced around the room. "I have one of them pointing at her head. She's gesturing at her head, near her temple on the right side. Does that mean anything to you?"

Kramer focused her eyes and faced Mrs. Waterson. The old woman was sitting up straighter, nodding. "In the accident, Myra hit her head. That was the wound that killed her—" The woman's voice was choked off by emotion.

A sharp look from her husband silenced any further explanation.

Kramer ignored him and listened for more.

"I see your other daughter. I'm gathering her name, which starts with the letter J, like Jennifer or Jenny. Yes, she's nodding. She says that she likes to be called Jenny. She keeps saying, 'Find a Jenny, find a Jenny.' I'm not sure what that means."

Mrs. Waterson ignored her husband and spoke loudly, a hidden strength from within forcing the words past her emotions. "When she was a kid, a phrase went, 'Find a penny, pick it up, all day long, you'll get good luck.' My daughters changed it to 'Find a Jenny …'"

Kramer wondered if Mr. Non-Believer Waterson was coming around yet. How could Kramer possibly know that if she wasn't actually speaking with his daughter?

"They're also saying sorry for something," Kramer added. "I see a boat, a dock, and—wait, yes, I see a cottage of some kind. They want to apologize for taking the boat out —" Kramer stopped as the image shattered. Her head shot back in response to the violence.

That powerful third entity was back and demanding she listen to him.

Her arm yanked sideways as Mr. Waterson ripped his hand away, breaking the circle.

"What is this?" he shouted at her. "What do you think you're doing? Anyone with two days' notice and a good private detective could've discovered that my *twin* daughters died in a boating accident at the cottage. You probably found out from your investigative digging that they weren't supposed to take the boat out, and that's why they're sorry." He rose from the table. "Tell us, who have you been talking to? Are any of my neighbors in on this?"

Kramer was taken aback. The third entity had forced its way in and was now shouting at her consciousness, which she was avoiding with all her concentration, and now her client was shouting at her, voicing untruths and disbeliefs.

"Mr. Waterson," Kramer said, releasing Mrs. Waterson's hand and rising to her feet. "I assure you that no one is trying to scam you. This information is learned firsthand"—she pointed at the table—"as we sit here. I knew nothing of you except your last name until you walked through that door and sat down in my kitchen. You must disperse your anger and retake the circle for this to work. Allow me to talk to your daughters some more. They have something urgent to tell me."

"I won't have it," he stated. "Come on, Margaret, we're leaving." He tugged on her shoulder, but his wife remained seated.

"Margaret?" he tried again. "What are you doing? You want to listen to more of this hogwash?"

Mrs. Waterson adjusted herself in her seat to glance up at him. "I have lost my two daughters and, along with them, my will to live. If they are here, with us in this room, as I believe they are, this may be my last chance to talk to them until I die and pass over to where they are. I have come here with a purpose, and I intend to stay to see that purpose through. As far as I'm concerned, you can do as you will. But know this —you will stop interrupting this kind woman and allow us to continue our session."

After a moment of gawking at her, the indecision battling his anger all over his face, Mr. Waterson sat back down and dropped his hand onto the table.

Kramer closed her eyes, refocused on Alweane, and said a silent prayer, asking her to control or eliminate the third entity.

The twins were clearly agitated by something. They started by sending an apology again and then explained why they were at the cottage that day.

Kramer opened her eyes. Now she knew what was wrong with Mr. Waterson. His denial, anger, and disbelief were rooted in whether or not this reading was authentic. He was terrified that it might be because if it was and the truth came out, his life was over, too.

It all became clear in seconds as the twins explained

everything.

"Mr. Waterson, is there something you want to tell us?" Kramer asked. "You know, before I explain what your daughters just recited to me."

He removed his hand again and glared at her. His fear now boiled over into a red zone of anger. As his energy raged across the table at her, she wondered for the first time if she was in danger.

"What gives you the right?" He breathed the words as much as he spoke them. "I only agreed to this because I knew it was hokey pokey bullshit."

Mrs. Waterson gasped. He paid her no mind.

"There's no way you are actually talking to dead folk. You take our money, research us, and then pretend to talk to our daughters. You've got some nerve, miss."

Kramer didn't miss a beat. What the twins told her caused hatred for Mr. Waterson unequaled by anything she'd encountered before that moment.

"I've just been informed that your nickname in grade school was Nine Doors. Is that true, Mr. Waterson? Who besides your lovely wife here would know that was your nickname until grade seven? It stood for Nicky Nicky Nine Doors, the game you played back then. You were the best at it." Kramer couldn't keep the disgust out of her voice.

Her words had hit a nerve. The Watersons exchanged a glance. They both knew how real this was now.

Alweane warned Kramer to ease the tension from the session because when the truth came out, Kramer didn't want the trouble, only justice.

"Are you ready to listen to everything else I've been

told?" she asked.

Mr. Waterson shook his head, seemingly making up his mind.

"No," he growled through clenched teeth. "I will not subject myself to this tirade from a charlatan anymore. You have made a fool of an old man. I'm leaving. Are you coming, Margaret?"

"Wait for me in the car," Mrs. Waterson said without hesitation or looking up at him.

Clearly surprised, he stepped back, staring down at her, then spun on his heels and strode to the door. Within seconds, he'd put on his shoes and stormed out, slamming the door behind him.

Mrs. Waterson shook her head. "I'm so sorry for my husband's behavior. I had to move mountains to get him to come today. As you may have noticed, he associated this with talking to the devil. You understand, yes?"

Kramer nodded. "I think it goes deeper than that." She paused because that *fucking* third entity was screaming at her from the living room area now.

This wasn't a haunting. She knew the difference. This being, this entity had something to say, but they were too strong and forceful about it. Scary strong, as Kramer told Alweane. She was so resilient that even her guide couldn't keep them away.

"Your husband, Mr. Waterson, is living in fear," Kramer started. "Are you ready for what I have to tell you?"

Mrs. Waterson nodded.

"Ma'am," Kramer said, wanting to offer her one more out. "Are you sure? You won't like what I have to say."

"Please. Tell me. I can't leave here without knowing."

Kramer stared at the table a moment. Mrs. Waterson was right. It was her duty to pass on the information.

She raised her gaze and stared at Mrs. Waterson, who had begun to cry. "Your husband kidnapped your daughters and forced them to the cottage that fateful day four summers ago."

Mrs. Waterson was nodding now. "I had suspected so. The night before they disappeared, Myra said she was sorry, but she had to tell me something important." Mrs. Waterson looked down at her lap, her lower lip trembling. "Myra said that Jenny was coming home the next day from her trip to Washington and that they would tell me everything together. I never got to hear what they wanted to tell me. The next day, their bodies were found in the lake. The boat they'd allegedly stolen had capsized." She met Kramer's gaze, her eyes watered over. "My babies had both drowned. To this day, I never understood why they went to the cottage."

Kramer reached across the table to hold onto Mrs. Waterson's hands. She needed to focus. That strong entity was in the kitchen now, moving around, trying to knock things over. Its attempt to get her attention was working her past fear of the unknown into anger of the known.

Kramer cleared her throat loudly to distract that crazy entity. "At this point, I don't know what, or even if, the police can do anything for you now. If you want to file a complaint, you can stay here and use my phone. If that would keep you safe, then I welcome it."

"Just tell me. Did my husband kidnap my girls to kill them?"

Kramer shook her head in the negative. "No, he didn't want to kill them. He wanted to silence them, though. The secret they were to share with you would've ruined your marriage. Would you prefer to hear it, or are you content with letting the past stay in the past?"

A yellow Frisbee flew over her head, catching her eye. It happened so suddenly that Kramer jerked away from her client. She looked at Mrs. Waterson, who hadn't moved but stared back at her wide-eyed.

"I'm sorry. Someone else is here, and they're quite powerful. Sometimes, when I call upon the other side, I risk inviting a strong presence to the table. A third entity has joined us with a message for me, but they're too powerful, and the message too grim." Kramer shook her shoulders and exhaled. "I'm sorry, you were about to answer my question."

After seeing nothing unusual, Mrs. Waterson glanced around the room, looked back at Kramer, and tried to smile. "I want to know what my daughters died trying to tell me."

Without hesitation, Kramer told her.

"When your daughters were five, your husband fathered another child with a woman two doors down from your house. A Ms. Sanchez or something like that. When your twins turned twenty-two years of age, they discovered his secret. Their seventeen-year-old brother from another mother came over from next door to tell them. He arrived with his thirty-year-old mother. Do you know what this means?"

Mrs. Waterson nodded, tears crawling down her cheeks. "It means that my husband cheated on me. This is something I've suspected over the years. I just never got enough nerve to leave."

"Not only that, it means your husband had sex with a thirteen-year-old girl and got her pregnant. Her mother, at the time, was undocumented and didn't reveal her father's identity. Mrs. Waterson, your husband didn't just cheat; he committed a serious crime. Your daughters wanted to tell you because this Sanchez woman wanted to press charges. When your daughters were found dead the next day, Mrs. Sanchez and her son remained silent about the affair and moved away in fear for their own lives. Your daughters' deaths were an accident; that part is true. But they were at the cottage because your husband was going to try to convince them to stay quiet. So …"

The third entity shouted so loud in her face one of the candles on the table blew out.

Kramer turned toward whoever it was and shouted, "Enough!"

Mrs. Waterson reared back, wiping at her tears. She pushed up off the table and bumped into the counter, knocking over an incense stick.

"I'm sorry about that interruption," Kramer said. "I know how this may look. I didn't mean to shout into empty air, but I assure you something was there." She paused for a moment. "Are you okay?"

"Yes." She pointed at the front door. "I need to go deal with this family problem my way. I thank you for your time, Ms. Kay."

A soft breeze flowed through the room, knocking out the other candle. Then, the kitchen was lost to darkness. By memory, Kramer rose from the table and yanked open the curtains by the window.

"What was that?" Mrs. Waterson asked. "How did that happen? Was that my girls?"

"Please, just ignore it. Are you sure you'll be okay?"

Mrs. Waterson moved toward the door and slipped into her shoes. "Thank you again," she said, nodding. "Good day."

And like that, she was gone.

"Spooked the shit out of you, didn't it?" Kramer turned around and stared back into her kitchen. "Who the hell are you, and what do you want? You can't hover around my readings like this anymore. It's too distracting and can be scary."

The entity rushed her, sending images into her consciousness.

Los Angeles. Downtown leveled. Thousands dead.

She closed her eyes, and a timeline formed in her mind's eye.

All of this was going to happen within a week or two.

Then she saw something that made her grasp her stomach to avoid throwing up. A dark-haired woman came into view, mangled and covered in blood. This woman was definitely dead. What caught Kramer's attention was the locket around her neck—her locket.

Kramer gasped.

The dead woman was herself.

This was a premonition of her own death, something she'd never seen before, nor did she ever think she'd be given the privilege of seeing.

She opened her eyes to rid the image from her mind, but it lingered. She clutched at the wall for support.

"Why?" she gasped, then started to cry. "Why show me this? What can I do? You expect me to …" she sobbed, caught herself, swallowed, and tried again. "You expect me to try and stop this? I can't change the future at this level. I don't want to know how I die …"

She moved over to the kitchen counter and turned the kettle back on. Then, deciding against a tea, she flicked it off and opened the liquor cabinet. After pouring herself a tall whisky, she retired to the living room.

"So what if I die in a week or two? Who cares?"

She held the whisky glass, her hands shaking, then sipped a mouthful.

A name was whispered in her ear.

Jacob.

She was supposed to call a man named Jacob. Save Jacob first. That was step one.

"What the hell does that mean, and who's Jacob?"

The yellow Frisbee floated by her face again. This time, it didn't startle her as much. She took another large pull from her whisky and looked in the corner from where the Frisbee had come.

A boy of about ten years of age stood there looking back.

He watched her for an entire minute, then lifted upward and disappeared from view.

Kramer drank the rest of the contents of her glass in one swallow.

Chapter 2

Officer Jamie Dent hadn't seen this much rain in years. The last thing he wanted was an accident with the crazy guy in the back seat.

He slowed down and turned the wipers to the faster mode. At the speed he'd been going, the rain sounded like little machine gun bursts on the windshield, blasting uncontrollably in a staccato rhythm.

"Heh, Cop, why don't you pull over and take a break? This rain will let up soon enough."

Officer Dent glanced in the rearview mirror at the man in the back.

Steven Wallace caught a lucky break when the judge said he'd drop the charges if Wallace agreed to detox and rehab. And now, en route to the Amy Greg Detox facility, Wallace sat there acting smug and content. Whether he was an addict or not didn't matter to Officer Dent. All that mattered to him was delivering the addict and heading home out of the rain.

"I asked you a question," Wallace said. "You gonna pull over or what?"

Officer Dent pressed down on the gas pedal.

"Why would I pull over?" Officer Dent asked. "You can't escape. The doors unlock from the outside. Or is it the rain? You afraid of a little rain?"

Wallace leaned forward, squinting out the windshield. "You can't see where you're going. It's dark, and your windshield is covered as soon as the wipers slide over it." Wallace leaned back in his seat. "A deer could walk out in front of us, and bam"—Steve clapped his hands hard, making Officer Dent jolt in his seat—"That's what I'm talking about. You smack a deer and go off the road, then what will I do? Huh? I'm locked in the back seat like a prison cell. What if you rolled the car, you're knocked out, and the car catches fire? You tell me, big cop. I'd die in here."

"Just sit tight. Nothing's going to happen. We aren't going to hit anything, and I'm not stopping. You're being admitted to the Amy Greg facility whether you like it or not."

Wallace can fight drug dealers and sell dope to kids, but he's afraid of the rain. Dent shook his head. Maybe the guy was crazy, and that's why he was always on drugs.

An explosion of noise made Officer Dent jump in his seat, a short yelp escaping his lips. The noise had originated from inside the cruiser. He'd tugged on the steering wheel slightly and had to adjust carefully on the slick road to keep them off the shoulder or, worse—the ditch.

Once they were back in the center of the road and nothing obstructed his headlights, Officer Dent glanced in the mirror at Wallace's smiling face.

"What the fuck was that?"

"I'm just playin' is all." He shrugged one shoulder. "I hit the Plexiglas with my cuffed hands to see how loud it would be in the car. Jeez, these handcuffs sure make a lot of noise." Wallace laughed.

"For someone afraid of the rain and the slippery conditions, that was an extremely stupid move." Officer Dent turned on the radio. Bruce Springsteen came through singing "Born in the USA."

"I'm not afraid of no little rain. You take that back." The cocky attitude was gone, replaced with a sad little boy routine. "I say, I say, you take that back."

"Just shut up," Dent yelled. "We're almost at your new home, so just shut the fuck up for the rest of the trip."

"I tell you what." Steve started up again in an altogether different voice. "You pull over. Tell them I was acting crazy, like, totally insane, and you couldn't control me. I started touching you in places you didn't want to be touched, and the next thing you know, I'm gone. There, poof, out of your hands, out of your mind. Isn't that how the sang goes?"

Officer Dent ignored Wallace. He had to. Otherwise, he would pull over and hurt the man in the back seat.

He'd driven this route so many times he knew the cut-off to the large detox center was coming up soon, but it was so damn hard to see with this rain.

"Okay, I got it," Wallace continued from the back seat. "You want me to touch you. Not just run away, but touch you in special places. So, okay, pull over, my fucker. Let's do this." Steve smacked the Plexiglas again.

Officer Dent reached over to the passenger seat and felt

around in the darkness for his smokes. When his hand alighted on the small container, he picked them up. After manipulating one to the edge of the pack, he glanced in the mirror at the prisoner.

"You want a cigarette first?"

"Sure," Steve said, leaning forward to take the proffered smoke through a hole in the Plexiglas.

Officer Dent smashed the brake pedal to the floor in that same instant.

As he did, his prisoner shot forward and smacked his face into the barrier between the front and the back seat, making an even louder noise than his hands had previously.

Steven Wallace moaned as he rubbed his forehead. Lucky for him, the cuffs were applied at the front. A large bump was already forming in the center of his forehead, and blood seeped out of the split skin.

"Damn, sorry about that. We almost missed the turn. Looks like we're here."

Officer Dent backed up the car about ten feet and then turned onto the Amy Greg Detox Center's main grounds.

"That's fucked up, man," Wallace mumbled. "I can't believe you did that. I'm gonna file a complaint. You're finished, asshat, you're fucking finished."

"I have no idea what you're talking about, crazy man. You banged your head against the barrier, demanding I let you go. Besides, I got ten years on the force, and you were just declared a dope addict. Tell me, who's gonna believe you?" Then he added, "Fuckin' idiot."

Dent stopped at the main entrance under a large canopy. It was past eight in the evening, and the place looked pretty quiet. Dent opened his door and ran around to unlock the back door on the passenger side.

He looked in at Steve. "Now, don't make me want to use my Taser on you. I mean, I'd like to, but I'm not feeling the paperwork tonight. So, I'll give you the choice. Come out of the car and act as normal as you can, or I will Tase you."

He stood back up, hand on his Taser, and waited. Steven Wallace exited slowly, acting crippled on account of his hands cuffed and half his face a mask of blood now.

"Damn, head wounds sure bleed a lot, eh?" Dent smiled.

He grabbed Steve's arm and led him in the front doors. A lone reception desk sat in the center of the main foyer. Usually, someone was sitting there, but tonight, the chair was empty.

"Damn, now what?" Wallace asked. "Maybe you gonna have to let me go after all. Nobody here to take me. So, what do you say, Cop? We done here?"

"You're not going anywhere, Steve. Just hold your horses. Someone's going to …"

A woman was walking toward them from one of the adjoining hallways.

"Can I help you—oh, my, what happened to you?"

The woman hustled over and stepped up to Steve.

"I'd like to file a complaint. This officer abused me."

"Ma'am." Officer Dent glared at her. "I'm releasing this prisoner into your care, but I advise you to have some help with him. He has committed violent crimes in his pursuit of narcotics and attempted to head-butt through the Plexiglas in my cruiser."

"Okay, Officer." She nodded. "That's what happened to

his head?"

Wallace made to protest, but Dent jerked his arm.

"Mr. Wallace was bashing it against the barrier in my cruiser, begging to be released. Now, if you call for someone to help take him, we can do the paperwork to sign him in."

"We had a small emergency, and most of our personnel are attending to that. Come on, we can put him in our holding room until they return."

She walked across the foyer and opened the door to a white room. Officer Dent led his prisoner in and maneuvered until his back faced the door. Then he undid the handcuffs and backed out of the room, shutting and locking the door behind him.

When peered through the small square window in the door, Wallace blew him a kiss and shouted, "I'm sure I'll see you again, pig."

Dent followed the woman back to the main desk, where he signed the release forms and headed for the door.

"Safe driving out there," the woman called after him.

Dent turned around and nodded. "Thanks. Have a good evening, and watch your back with that guy. He's a former CI. He might cause trouble."

Dent pushed the door open and stopped when he heard her voice once more.

"A CI?" she called. "What's that?"

He glanced back. "A criminal informant retired now."

The woman nodded, a new serious expression on her face.

Officer Dent stepped back out under the canopy, got in his car, and headed back into the city.

His job was done.

29

Chapter 3

THE GRIEF COUNSELOR SAID IT WOULD abate over time. Time heals all wounds, yet it hasn't healed this one for some reason.

Maria Lopez felt the grief of losing her husband like she had eternal flu symptoms. The grief stayed with her, holding her back from life, never easing the terrible grasp. She couldn't work, she couldn't play, she couldn't function. Her husband had been her life, and when he died, he took her soul, too.

What she saw staring back at her in the bathroom mirror was a ghost of the girl she used to know.

The woman in the mirror was still in love with John Tarkington, the man who took her away from a terrible upbringing in South America. The man who rescued her married her, adored her, cherished her.

Maria's husband, dead now for over a year, and still haunting her every dream, her every waking moment.

Her makeup was wrong, her hair off somehow, but she kept getting ready for her second last appointment with Dr. Kinsey. She had two meetings left to convince him that she was ready to break free from therapy. On her next appointment in two weeks, her last one, she would be finished with him. No more visits, no more therapy.

That's what she needed: no more therapy. It was seeing Dr. Kinsey, who kept bringing up the past, reminding her of all she had lost. That had to be it—the constant talking about it, the constant reminders.

Finished with the bathroom, she grabbed her blouse off the bed and continued dressing. After putting on her red heels, she strode into the living room and stared at the candles she'd lit earlier. They were withering and melting onto the wooden shelf where the altar to John sat.

It hit her then that she was just like the candles, using the wax to fuel the flame, but as the wax got used up, the flame would eventually die. Her life was the wax, her breath, the flame. One day, she would stop breathing and run out of wax, and then she could be with John.

The makeshift altar appeared unkempt, with the wax dripping the way it had. She needed to buy more candles and fix it up when she got home. Her husband deserved better than that.

She turned away, grabbed her purse, and headed for the door, but something stopped her. It was like someone was watching her. The creepy feeling stayed with her, oozing into her shoulders.

Maria shuddered a moment, then turned and scanned the living room. With her right hand, she crossed herself and stared at the altar. As she did, one of the candle's flames spun in the air as if someone had blown on it. Then, as fast as it flared, it extinguished itself.

She gasped, her hand racing to cover her mouth. Wildly, Maria studied the immediate area for movement but saw nothing. If someone was here, she couldn't see them.

That meant only one thing—it was John.

"John, oh John, is it you?" Maria whispered.

Nothing happened. She received no response, only silence.

What stage is this? The acceptance stage or the bargaining stage?

This was real. She felt it. She knew it. John was with her. He watched over her. He'd never leave her, even in death.

"I love you, John. I really do, and one day, I will come and spend eternity with you."

As she spoke, another candle flickered.

"Oh John ..."

The candle sputtered out. The altar was unlit now, eerie in its darkness.

Maria shivered once more as she walked out the door, whispering a quiet prayer to a God of mercy to ease the pain in her heart.

Maybe the therapist would believe her, maybe he wouldn't. He kept referring to the five stages of grief and how she needed to have a natural procession through them. It had taken some time, but Maria convinced him she was in the final stage. Their meetings were coming to an end because of that. She needed to get away from him anyway because he trolled through her memories, stealing her childhood from her and replacing it with a dark cloud, all in the name and interest of healing her.

Maria didn't want to heal. She wanted her husband. She wanted her life back. Or she wanted to die. Whichever one brought her closer to John was the one she desired the most.

None of those options had anything to do with therapy or Dr. Kinsey.

Maria got in her car and headed to the Amy Greg Center, intent on finishing her second last appointment and then going shopping for new candles.

Her dead husband deserved more respect.

Chapter 4

STEVEN WALLACE WOKE WITH A SPLITTING headache. His first few moments of consciousness were foggy and unclear. He thought he was waking in the jail where they had been holding him.

Then, it all came back in waves. All of it, even the cheap shot the cop gave him in the cruiser.

He touched his forehead. A goose egg the size of a golf ball had ballooned just below his hairline. The area where the skin had split was raw and sore, with remnants of crusted and clotted blood lining the area.

"That motherfucker …" he mumbled to himself.

He sat up slowly, mindful of his movements to avoid exacerbating the headache. The room looked like a minimum security jail cell. The walls were an ugly blue. The beds had better mattresses, though, but none of that mattered because Steven Wallace wasn't planning on spending another night in this joint.

Someone knocked on the door, startling him. Keys jangled outside, the lock clicked, and then two men dressed all in white escorted a female into the room.

"You got something I can take for this headache?" Steve asked. "Man, does this bitch sting."

"Pharmaceuticals are distributed to patients as needed based on their program here at the Amy Greg facility." The woman stopped at the side of his bed, looking down at him. "Until you are formally checked in and examined, I cannot administer anything for you." She handed him a clipboard. "Please complete everything you can as best as possible, and we will be back in an hour to collect the forms. After that, lunch is being served in the cafeteria, and later in the afternoon, we have a Bingo game that you might want to attend as long as you don't cause anyone any trouble. Would there be anything else, Mr. Wallace?"

"So formal," Steve said, shaking his head. He leaned back on the bed. "Look, I didn't do what they're saying I did. I plea bargained to get in here. But remember"—he raised a hand in the air, index finger held high—"I did not do what they claim I did. So, let a fellow American deal with the head pain. Give me a fucking Tylenol or some shit Advil. Either that or give me a break and let me walk to the corner store to get some on my own."

"There will be no leaving this facility, nor will there be any violations of our code of conduct and rules, Mr. Wallace. It's all in the forms. Now, please read and fill out those forms, and we will return in one hour for them."

"Ahh, come on. You gotta be kidding me. I'm in pain here. It's your job to do something about it."

"One hour," she said and stepped back, spun around, then strode between the two men in white. A second later, after staring down at Wallace, they backed out and secured the door behind them.

"You're gonna pay for that, bitch. Shit, I didn't even get your name."

Steve recoiled his arm, then threw the clipboard. It hit the corner and snapped in half, dropping to the floor.

"Oh shit, now I'm gonna be in trouble for wrecking institute property." Wallace laughed, then stopped abruptly as it hurt his head too much.

An idea came to him as he lay back, his eyes closed. As soon as his head would allow, he got off the bed, picked up the papers attached to the clipboard, and started writing. When he was finished, he snapped the clipboard into several pieces, looking for the exact size and shape to make a shiv. After careful craftsmanship, Steve had fashioned a shiv with a pointed end that was a little longer than his grip so it could be concealed well, with the business end still sticking out enough to do proper damage.

He had roughly ten minutes left until they returned for the forms.

Wouldn't they be surprised with what he had waiting for them?

Sometime today, Steven Wallace would walk out of this facility a free man, and he would go off the grid and disappear for good.

No one would find him this time.

No one.

Chapter 5

DAN MORGAN SET HIS NOVEL DOWN and yawned, his eyes watering at how tired he felt. Some novels kept him up all night.

His wife had retired over an hour before, but he wanted to sneak in one more chapter—which turned into ten more. Only a Worthington novel could do that to him.

After turning off the lights, he headed upstairs, brushed his teeth, and slipped quietly and softly into bed beside her, careful not to wake her.

With his iPad on the lowest light, Dan flipped through the news until his eyes grew heavy, and he turned it off.

One in the morning gave him six to seven hours of sleep as they usually woke early for coffee on the back deck.

In their usual way of sleeping together, Dan angled in and cuddled his wife, who was facing the wall.

In minutes, he drifted off.

The short clinking sound came from a dream, but

something registered in his head, and his eyes popped open.

Was it a dream? Or did he actually hear something in the house?

He opened his eyes in the darkness and tilted away from his wife to listen to the now silent house.

After half a minute without breathing to hear better, he angled into her again, thinking it must have been in his head.

The light in the bedroom flicked on, startling him awake.

He jumped up, gasping for air, when someone in a black costume shoved his shoulder down into the bed.

The man's fist connected with his face.

And now Patricia, his wife, was screaming.

More people filled the room.

"What the fuck—" He struggled, but strong arms restrained him.

Another shot to the face cut off any more pleas.

Two men dragged him from the bed. He hit the floor hard, making him wince and cry out. His face was on fire, and they were grabbing at him again, shoving him onto his stomach before he even had a chance to respond or defend himself.

Patricia's screams were cut off.

Dan struggled under their grip, then tried to flip back over, but another fist to his cheek all but silenced the fight inside him.

He'd never been a violent man, never fought physically after sixth grade, and was outnumbered and outmuscled.

His arms were yanked behind him, his wrists tied with enormous speed.

Then they flipped him over and yanked him to his feet all

in one fluid movement.

The adrenaline, the fear coursing through his system, was enough that his legs wouldn't hold him up, and he dropped onto the bed, moaning.

A monster of a man was holding Patricia, one arm around her chest, the other covering her mouth.

His wife's eyes were bloodshot with sleep and wide with fear.

Regrets and thoughts of what he could've done differently raced through his mind. Even though he was a soft man of science, a lecturer at the Fraser Institute, from somewhere within him came a burst of something akin to a protective alpha. He wanted to hurt all these men and make them pay for what they had done to his wife. They frightened her and intimidated her, and she was made to watch as her husband was beaten and tied like cattle.

The urge to hurt them all and escape was just that—an urge. There was no way he could get the upper hand, nor did he have any idea how that could be achieved, even if he wanted to.

"Dan Morgan," one of the men said. It sounded like he barked the name.

Dan nodded quickly.

"You come with us. We'll explain later."

He nodded again. "My wife—my wife stays here?"

The man shook his head. "Wife comes, too. Compliance."

The man holding Patricia moved toward the door, literally lifting her off the carpeted bedroom floor as he walked. In his thick arms, she seemed to be weightless.

Hands grabbed him and forced him to his feet. He stumbled, but they didn't let go. Moments later, they were all standing at the front door.

"Why?" Dan mumbled, his voice shaking in fear. "Why are you doing this to us?"

"Shut up," one of the men shouted. "I will beat you unconscious."

Dan registered the man's accent this time. How did he not notice it upstairs?

"You go with us. Help us. Then come home. No one gets hurt. You refuse us, you die. Understood?"

Dan nodded vigorously.

The man holding Patricia opened the door.

Just outside, two stretchers had been set up at the door, an ambulance parked at the curb. The large man tied Patricia to one of them while the other two men shoved Dan on the second stretcher and secured him bodily to it with straps.

"Just do as they say," Dan said to Pat.

The large man ripped a piece of duct tape from a roll and applied it to Patricia's mouth. Miraculously, she hadn't screamed once after the man's hand came away from her mouth.

Then Dan's stretcher was being wheeled toward a waiting ambulance.

What the hell? Who brings an ambulance to a kidnapping?

He struggled to look behind him. Patricia's stretcher was coming now, too.

In the doorway of his house, a man in a long coat stood watching them all leave. Dan focused on that man until he couldn't see him anymore.

Why was someone staying behind? Wasn't that risky? What if a neighbor saw the kidnapping and called the police?

Once he was loaded and the back doors were secured, the man who had punched him before took a seat beside him.

Then he lifted off his mask to reveal his face.

Dan had watched the movies. He was able to identify the man now.

That wasn't good. That wasn't good at all.

"Night," the man said.

The ambulance started moving at the same time the man drove a fist into Dan's cheek, effectively knocking him out with the force of the one violent punch.

Chapter 6

Bryce Jacob strode through the police department, nodding at colleagues as he headed for Bill McGregor's office door. Most cops hated a summons to the sergeant's office, but Jacob was past all that. Sergeant Bill McGregor didn't intimidate him anymore or make Jacob feel less job security. McGregor was all bark and no bite, and his bark could be ferocious, but so was Bryce Jacob's.

He stopped outside Sarge's door and listened briefly, then knocked.

The low sound of the sarge inviting him in trickled through the door.

Jacob pushed it open and stepped inside the lion's den, as his fellow officers called it.

"Take a seat," McGregor said in his usual gruff tone. It was like the guy was always perturbed about something, as if he'd just finished an argument on the phone.

Jacob inhaled deeply to calm his nerves as his patience

was thin. Then he eased the door closed and lumbered over to one of the two chairs, where he plopped down to stare at the Sarge. While he waited, Sergeant McGregor scratched a match across the top of his desk, lit a cigarette, blinked away the smoke several times, and then moved to the window to stare down at the street below.

There was no point in reminding the man of the NO SMOKING signs and rules set forth by the department. Better to wait in silence for whatever bullshit McGregor wanted to chat about.

"We've got something sensitive to discuss," the sarge said, turning from the window to look at Jacob. "You know I like you, Detective Jacob. You remind me of a younger me."

Yeah, right. Just not as stupid. "I'm sure there are some differences," Jacob whispered, trying to keep the disdain out of his voice.

McGregor pivoted to face Jacob and drew on his cigarette, allowing the smoke to envelop his face, then he stepped closer, pushing through the smoke.

Bryce Jacob suppressed a laugh at how ridiculous the man looked.

"I know we don't always see eye to eye." McGregor held up a finger. "I also know when that changed." He inhaled the cigarette, then blew out smoke rings like a teenager in the smoking section of a high school.

Jacob decided to bite on the lure. "When did we stop seeing eye to eye?"

"When your son was killed."

Jacob sat back and crossed his arms. Dangerous territory for a conversation, especially from the man in front of him, a man he didn't respect.

It had been a year. Lance Jacob was only a ten-year-old boy when he was run down by an old Camaro near the beach while Jacob and Lance were hanging out and playing catch. There were many clues on the case but no arrests. The case was either being fumbled or directly neglected, which pissed off Jacob—and they would never let him work the case, so there's that. Whatever the situation was, Jacob had taken a leave of absence to grieve. Although he was pursuing his own leads, he was working his own case with CIs and fellow officers. Yet, they'd routinely shut him out as his colleagues feared reprisals from Sergeant McGregor. After nine months off the force and not much to go on yet, Jacob had decided to return and continue working his investigation on the inside.

So, without breathing life into the reason the sergeant and Jacob didn't get along anymore—which was because his son's murderers hadn't been apprehended yet—he kept his mouth shut. The man standing before him was in charge. The *fuck* stops here, is how Jacob saw it, and this man was full of excuses.

"I'm getting the feeling," McGregor continued, "that after you lost your son, you didn't grieve enough." He eyed him, waiting for a reaction, but Jacob didn't give him one. "Sure, you took off nine months, but you were seen time and again by my investigating officers trying to gather your own information." He held up his hand to ward off a response. "I know, I know, we've already covered that. I'm talking about your attitude since you got back. Frankly, it stinks." He puffed on his cigarette again, blowing smoke toward Jacob this time.

"We done here?"

"See what I mean?" McGregor shot up his hands. "You disrespect the fact that you're being dressed down by your superior officer by blowing off my comments as if I said the football game is on TV this weekend. It's not a big deal, right? Wrong! You're pissing people off, Jacob. You gotta fix it."

"Who am I pissing off? And if I am, fuck 'em. My son's dead, and I won't stop until I find out who did it."

McGregor moved to sit down behind his desk. He stared at Jacob through the cigarette smoke curling up from his clenched hands resting in front of his face. He always had to be so dramatic.

"Why fuck 'em? What makes you say that?"

"I'm doing my job. I'm a detective with a good arrest record. My son was murdered a year ago, and his murderers are still out there somewhere. Even though I work narcotics, I will do whatever I can to find the bastards who ran my son down, or I will hound the homicide detectives until they decide to find the driver of that Camaro. That's why fuck 'em. Because my search for justice isn't a popularity contest. I could give a flying fuck who likes me and who doesn't."

McGregor sat back and dragged on his smoke again. The room was rapidly filling with the acrid smell of Export 'A'.

"We're on the same side," McGregor said. "We're fighting the same guys. I can't have you fighting our guys, too. And what about these complaints of excessive force on a couple of arrests you've made recently? How do you want me to handle that?"

Jacob didn't reply. Those complaints were common. The

allegations of abuse were always being dealt with, and the sarge knew it. Routine shit, but here he was, bringing it up like it meant something. He was playing a game with him in order to calm him down. But being calm never found a murderer—calm didn't solve a case.

McGregor chuckled briefly. "Enough with the sour shit. It's good to have you back. Just take it easy. Lighten up a little out there, okay?"

Jacob nodded. *Not until I find who killed my son.*

"I got something I need you to do," McGregor added before Jacob could get to his feet. "You remember that junkie, Steven Wallace?"

"Yeah."

"He was dropped off last night at the Amy Greg Detox Facility. When he got there, he looked bad, all bloody and shit."

Jacob got to his feet, standing ramrod straight. "What happened?"

"He complained to the attendants there that the cop who dropped him off had done it intentionally. Something about him smashing his head."

"What do you want me to do?"

"Wallace was your arrest, your informant. Go to Amy Greg today and talk to him. See what you can find out. Then, take the rest of the day off. Cool out. Just chill."

"Visit a convicted druggie at the detox clinic to investigate a fellow officer? Is that what you're asking me to do?"

McGregor nodded, then jammed his cigarette in the ashtray, mashing the tip downward until the smoke stopped rising from it.

"No, I'm telling you." McGregor met his gaze, his face hardening. "Not asking."

"Isn't that internal affairs territory?" Jacob asked. "Why would I investigate a fellow officer?"

"Look, I know your department can do their jobs without you. Take the rest of the day off or the rest of the week. All I'm saying is, you gotta calm down sooner rather than later, or you may not have a job."

"You're bottom lining it for me?" Jacob asked. "Is that it, do this, or you're gone?"

"Listen to me. You're bugging a lot of people in the search for your justice when all the rest of us are doing our jobs the best we can. This isn't bottom-lining it for you. This isn't even a warning. This is an intervention. You're gonna lose your sanity hunting down phantom killers—"

A knock at the door silenced the sergeant.

Just in fucking time.

"Come in," McGregor shouted.

The break allowed Jacob to collect himself. The edge of an outrage had crept up on him. A rush of anger flowed through him, his hands clenched, and his forehead broke out in a sweat.

Detective Mike Spencer stuck his head in, saw Jacob, and nodded, then stared at the sergeant.

"Thought you'd want to hear this right away."

"Go on, Spencer, spill it."

"We may have caught a lucky break on the kidnapping of Dan Morgan and his wife from last night."

"Make it quick. I'm in a meeting here." McGregor's eyes

darted to Jacob.

Mike Spencer from homicide. Jacob had hounded him for the last couple of months about the murder of Lance Jacob files. Since he was a homicide detective, why was he working a kidnapping case?

Also, if he wasn't mistaken, the sarge was bothered about something more than just their meeting today. McGregor was worried, nervous, or agitated about something as if Jacob was getting close to the truth. But if so, wouldn't that be another solved case? Why would that bother McGregor? Who cared if the narcotics division, Detective Jacob, solved a murder case? Conflict of interest, or the fact that he was too close to the murder victim, didn't bother Jacob. He just wanted answers.

So why pull him off the case and onto some bullshit run out of the city? Why tell him to take more time off?

As Detective Spencer prattled on about some kidnapping, Jacob realized that there was more going on than he was privy to.

McGregor knew more than he was letting on, which put him on Jacob's radar.

Detective Jacob would learn what it was that Sergeant McGregor knew, or he'd beat it out of him.

Sometimes, men just didn't learn unless they were beaten. And sometimes, they were smarter than that.

Sergeant McGregor wasn't in that category.

Chapter 7

Steve heard the keys first, and then the door to his room shot open. The bed may offer comfort to the body, but his head had no reprieve from the incessant pounding it was enduring.

"Did you bring me painkillers?" he asked in a whisper. "Please tell me you did."

He opened his eyes. The same woman from earlier, the one who gave him the clipboard, stood over him, looking down. She'd only brought one orderly with her this time. The shiv hidden in his right hand comforted him. He contemplated using it now, then making a run for it even though his head felt like it was about to explode. The pain was so intense, though, that he needed to wait. Halfway down the hallway, he'd pass out from the pain if he got up too quickly, fought the orderly, and ran outside. When the right opportunity came, he would strike. Until then, he'd wait.

"As I mentioned before," the woman said. "Nothing can be administered until you are fully checked in and seen by our attending physician."

"That will be too late. Either my head will erupt off my shoulders, or the headache will be gone by then. I need something now."

"What happened to my clipboard? Why didn't you fill in the paperwork as requested?"

"You want my cooperation? Shit, man, I don't even know you. How about you cooperate with me first? On the back of those papers, I wrote out my complaint or statement or whatever the fuck they call it. That cop hit me last night when he delivered me here. The goose egg on my forehead is causing me a lot of pain. Once you file this complaint, maybe someone with more authority than you could come to see me, and then *maybe*, just maybe, I could have a painkiller."

"There's a chance I didn't make myself clear." She picked up the remaining pieces of the clipboard and handed them to the orderly. Then she glanced at the paperwork for a moment before meeting his gaze. "This is a detox center. Most people in attendance are here by choice, but we have people like you who are here due to a court order. You are in here because they don't feel you can make it on the outside until you've been rehabilitated, not to mention this is your sentence as described by the courts. You skipped out on jail time on the premise that you do our program." She moved closer to the bed. "While you're here, we will rehabilitate you whether you like it or not. Your attitude and smartass remarks only reveal the scared little boy inside trying to lash out at your supervisors. Your whole life has been about taking away the pain through denial of your addictions. We know that here." She folded the papers and stashed them in her white coat pocket. "Now that you don't have access to those addictions, you are frustrated. I get that. I understand it. You don't think that we see your kind in here all the time? Mr. Wallace, learn this and learn it quickly. The sooner you respect us, the sooner we'll respect you. If you want this to be hard, we can assign someone resembling a drill sergeant. He will turn your life into a detox boot camp. Or you can try the program willingly and allow us to help you. Either way, you are going to swallow this program and leave here clean, or you'll leave here like you came—in handcuffs on your way to jail. Either option is up to you."

"Is that the best you got, 'swallow this program'? Is that what they teach you at Shrink School? You've got to be kidding me." He laughed, then squinted at the pain. "Good luck trying this program shit on me. I don't perform well in group sessions. I'll get through my time here, then leave and score a hit and be done with this shit."

The woman moved back to the door, the man following close behind her.

"That's fine, Mr. Wallace, have it your way. But I'm telling you now, you won't like your stay here with that attitude. Tomorrow at six a.m., it all starts. Breakfast at seven a.m. You'll get the rest of your schedule after breakfast."

"At least we agree on one thing. I won't enjoy my stay here because I won't be here long enough to find out."

The woman exited his room and slammed the steel door so hard it made Steve reach for his temples in pain.

Next time, bitch. I will stab someone and leave. Next

time.

Whoever visited him next would open that door, and it wouldn't close until Steven Wallace stepped through it in order to leave the building.

Next time.

Chapter 8

"WITNESS STATEMENTS HELPED US ON THIS one," Detective Mike Spencer was saying.

Bryce Jacob had zoned him out for several minutes as Sergeant McGregor grilled the homicide cop on details. Originally, he'd asked him to make it quick, but now they were passing the five-minute mark. Perhaps McGregor didn't want to talk to Jacob anymore.

"Apparently," Spencer continued. "Morgan and his wife were removed by an ambulance, but their neighbor next door said she saw Dan's hands were bound while he was on the stretcher. At first, the neighbor figured there had been domestic violence, and they were securing him, but there were no visible wounds on either Morgan or his wife. Possible bruising on Dan's face, but they couldn't tell for sure. Then, when his wife came out on a stretcher, her hands were tied, too." The homicide cop glared at Jacob briefly, nodded slightly, and addressed the sergeant again. "The neighbor's house is so close that the dining room window looks right out onto the front porch of the Morgans' place. Now, here's the catch. The wife had duct tape on her mouth, and we've got two witnesses that would swear they saw weapons hidden under coats."

"Weapons?" McGregor asked.

Jacob sat up straighter.

"Yes, weapons. My question is, why kidnap a guy like Dan Morgan?"

"Who is this Morgan guy?" the sarge asked. "Why is he important?"

"He's the Fraser Institute of Technology scientist who wrote a non-fiction bestseller on sound waves. Apparently, the guy is the resident expert on everything sound-related to decibel ranges and the power of shock waves traveling through air and water. From what we've gathered, he's the ultimate American, too. When he's not working, he's hunting at his lodge."

"Would you kidnap this kind of guy if you were building a bomb, some sort of IED?"

Both men looked at McGregor. *What a strange question*, Jacob thought.

"Ah, maybe, I guess." Spencer shrugged. "You'd want a physicist or someone more hands-on. Why?"

"No reason, just working a theory from another case. Anything else?"

"Right after the ambulance pulled out before the neighbor closed the curtains, she saw a man exit the house and walk over to an older model Camaro. Then the fire started—"

Jacob shot up from his chair. "Did you get an ID on the car? A plate?"

"Jacob, take it easy," McGregor said. "Sit back down."

He ignored the sergeant and stared at the officer standing before him. "Did you?"

"Not yet, but we're working on it."

"Let me know when you do."

"Jacob, I said take it easy," McGregor shouted. "They'll let me know what they find out, and when we apprehend someone, we'll look at other possible cases they may be tied to. You know how this works. Now sit down because you and I aren't finished." McGregor turned back to Spencer as Jacob eased back into the chair. "Anything else?"

"The fire trucks arrived but couldn't get control of the fire before the house was razed. They managed to save both houses on the left and right, though. The Fire Marshall is on-site investigating it as we speak. Also, there weren't any reports of ambulances being called to that address from local hospitals."

"Okay, let me know when you get anything else." McGregor made a shooing motion. "Leave us. I need to finish with Detective Jacob here."

Where were the bodies in a kidnapping? Why would homicide be interested until they had a murder victim?

"Jacob, that little performance is exactly what I'm talking about. You don't have the authority to tell other cops to report to you. What do you think this is?"

"I'm only trying to find my son's murderer. We're cops. It's what we do. We're on the same side, so then we help each other out."

"You're not getting it, are you?" McGregor twirled his cigarette pack as if he wanted to pull another one out. "I'm not telling you this because I like to. I'm telling you to calm down because I have to cover my ass, too. You're a narcotics officer. Do your job in the drug unit and leave homicide alone. Let them do their jobs unimpeded by you."

Jacob steepled his fingers in front of his face. "Are we done here?"

"I guess so. You're not listening, and I'm telling you that it will cost you your job if you don't start—"

The phone on the sergeant's desk rang. He reached out and hit a button.

"Yes?"

"We just received a faxed written complaint from Steven Wallace at the Amy Greg Center. You said if anything from him came in to call you directly."

"Okay, good. I will be sending Detective Bryce Jacob out to meet with Mr. Wallace. Thanks." He released the button and looked back at Jacob. "There you go. Your assignment. Read the complaint, visit the detox center, and go home. You're done for the day."

Jacob got up and headed for the door. McGregor's booming voice made him turn around.

"Don't push this. Everything will work out, but if you push this, you could also be a casualty. So, ask yourself, would your son want that?"

Jacob opened the door, jumped through it, then slammed it shut before his anger got the better of him.

Something was going on. His gut told him someone was covering up information or withholding it, and whatever it was could be the key to solving his son's murder.

He didn't care if an informant got busted or a small-time dealer got taken down. Whoever was behind the killing of his son had to pay, and Jacob wasn't going to wait until a bigger fish was picked up to do it.

Almost everything that happened in his police department went through the sergeant. That meant if someone knew something here, the sarge also knew.

That meeting confirmed to Bryce that Sergeant Bill McGregor was hiding something.

And Jacob was determined to find out what it was. Whether he had a job after or not didn't matter.

Finding Lance Jacob's murderer was all that mattered to Bryce.

Chapter 9

The door opened without a knock, startling Wallace.

He shot his hand out to his right to cover the shiv lying on the bed beside him.

"Don't you people ever fucking knock? I mean, what the hell, man?"

To cover his sudden movement and garner whatever sympathy he could, Steve took his other hand and placed it on his forehead, moaning for effect.

The same woman—again!—from earlier stood over him. Although, this time, she was alone. They must have determined he was safe and not a risk after all.

"I've emailed your complaint to the authorities. I was told that an officer will come by soon to take a statement from you in person. A Detective Jacob, if I'm not mistaken."

"No, not him, please, not him."

"Why not? Why does it matter who comes to take your statement?"

"He's my arresting officer. Practically beat me up when he witnessed a transaction. He's a rough cop, stronger and meaner than the guy who drove me here last night, and he seems eternally pissed off. He won't listen to my statement, take me seriously, or ever try to understand. You've wasted your time reaching out."

"You wanted them to know, so I did as you asked. I didn't *request* him, but that's who they're sending. In the meantime, can I get you anything while you wait other than painkillers?"

"Sure, I could use a glass of water."

"That I can do." She spun away. "I'll be right back."

The woman stepped out of the room. Steve got up, positioned himself on the other side of the door, and got the shiv ready. He only had to wait a few minutes before the door opened again, and the woman stepped inside.

She stopped a few feet from the bed and turned around. "Mr. Wallace?"

Steve shot forward before she was turned around enough to face him, wrapped an arm around her neck, and pulled her into him.

"You will not scream," he said, raising the shiv high enough for her to see it. Then he jabbed it at her neck. She whimpered once in response, one hand on his forearm, the other still holding the water. "If you scream, I will slice your throat open and still leave this place. Don't die for my freedom, bitch. Do I make myself clear?"

The woman nodded quickly, indicating to Steve that she was more than scared and compliant.

Then she tossed the water over her shoulder and into his

face.

He gasped as his eyes closed. His grip was lost as she dropped to the floor. He blinked rapidly and kicked out, connecting to some part of her.

The woman groaned. She was crawling toward the door.

The pain in his head made it feel like he'd been shot and was fighting with the shooter.

No choice now, though. He was in this until it was over. Handcuffs or freedom.

He dove on her as she got to the door, and they fell sideways into the doorframe. She yelled out for help, but he was able to clamp a hand over her mouth.

Then he yanked backward, and whether he cracked her back or a bone snapped, he couldn't tell, but she fell onto his stomach, the shiv back at her neck.

He pushed it in a notch deeper until a warm liquid ran through his fingers.

"Try something like that again, whore, and I'll end it." He blinked away the rest of the water and pushed her over so they could get to their feet. "Now, direct me to the nearest exit."

Chapter 10

Maria was two miles from the Amy Greg facility when she noticed an unmarked cruiser following her. Her stomach clenched at the notion that she'd be pulled over. Did she make a wrong turn? Was she driving too fast and didn't notice?

The speedometer read that she was going five miles over the limit, so she eased off the pedal slightly and allowed the car to coast to the speed limit.

Maria placed both hands on the wheel and focused on her driving. She hated being followed by cops. Even if she'd done nothing wrong, it always made her feel guilty, like they had a purpose to follow her.

The turn-off for the driveway that led to the Amy Greg came into view. Maria put on her blinker and scanned her mirrors.

The cop's blinker came on, too.

Maybe he was coming to visit someone or something.

The Amy Greg facility had two wings. One was a detox center, and one was a regular facility where many psychiatrists and psychologists practiced out of small offices with larger rooms for group therapy sessions. More and more people need help these days, so the entire facility was designed to do just that.

From her mirrors, it appeared the driver was alone.

Wouldn't he have done it by now if he wanted to pull her over? Even knowing this, her stomach didn't let up with the butterflies.

Seconds later, she made the turn, drove up the long driveway, and found a parking spot near the front. Maria turned off her car and spun around in her seat to see what the cop car was doing.

The cruiser eased in beside her vehicle and stopped. The driver of the cruiser looked over, smiled, and nodded, then proceeded to get out.

That made her feel better. He wasn't pursuing her after all. It had to be official business only. Also, she felt reassured that if he were acting on a complaint, he wouldn't appear so calm and relaxed. There would be a sense of urgency in his manner.

With her purse in hand, Maria opened her door and stepped out of her vehicle.

The sun was still high, the lush greens and gorgeous flowers near the main entrance standing out in the bright light. She checked over her shoulder as she approached the main doors with the cop several feet behind her. The area was surrounded by a huge forest, with the closest building about seven hundred yards away, just across a small river that flowed through the facility's grounds.

When she reached the main door, the cop jumped ahead and held it open for her. She gave him a nod, entered the main foyer, showed her pass to the receptionist, and started down the hallway to the left leading to the staircase. Her therapist was on the second floor of the other building, and there was a neat, elevated walkway between the two wings that would take her over to his office. She was ten minutes early for her appointment, giving her time to stop in the walkway and snap pictures.

Ever since John was killed, she tried to find beauty wherever she could.

Near the end of the hallway, someone screamed.

Chapter 11

Detective Jacob ambled up to the receptionist after holding the door for the attractive Latino woman. He watched her head toward the long corridor on the left as he pulled out his badge and stepped up to the desk.

"Detective Bryce Jacob here to see a patient named Steven Wallace regarding a complaint."

"Steven Wallace, Steven Wallace," the woman whispered under her breath as she scanned a computer screen with her finger. "Got him. He just checked in last night, so he's in room 104."

"Can you direct me which way that is?"

The receptionist pointed toward the Latino woman. "Follow her. About halfway down, it's on the left."

When Bryce looked where she was pointing, movement caught his eye. It was like something moved near the floor halfway down. Jacob studied the area but saw no movement except the Latino woman still walking toward the double doors at the end of the corridor.

"Officer, room 104 is that way," the receptionist said as he stopped and stared in a daze.

A woman screamed for help.

The Latino woman spun around and stopped near the end of the hall.

Jacob started running as a man holding a woman around the neck stepped out of the room. They backed down the hall toward the double doors, the man half dragging the woman.

Jacob was catching up quickly as they weren't making good progress.

He flipped the clasp on his holster and withdrew his weapon. Within seconds, he was ten steps away from them.

Before he ordered the guy to release the woman, their eyes met.

Steven Wallace.

His face was so wet it looked like the guy had sweat several buckets already in detox. But what set Bryce off was the blood trickling from the woman's neck.

"Let her go, Wallace."

"Fuck you, pig."

They'd almost made it to the double doors when the woman who was being held grabbed Wallace's arm, wrenched it downward, and then spun her body away from him and jumped aside.

One minute, she was subdued in his grasp with something sharp cutting her skin, and the next, she was standing several feet away from him.

Steve swiped at her with whatever was in his hand, missing as the woman jumped away and ran toward Jacob, then behind him.

"Wallace, don't do it," Jacob yelled. "Drop the weapon. I don't want to have to put you down."

He was fifteen feet away and closing fast. To Jacob's dismay, the Latino woman had stopped at the doors to gawk at the action. Steve spun around, bolted the ten feet to her, grabbed the woman, and held her at the neck.

"Leveled up," Steve shouted. "New victim achieved. Stay back, or I will slice her throat open."

"This isn't a video game, asshole." Jacob slowed his pace and got as close as he dared. Less than ten feet separated them. The Latino woman appeared to be taking this well.

Feet pounded the floor behind Jacob. He held up an arm. "Everyone, stay back." He moved a few feet closer to Wallace. "Steve, what are you doing? Do you know the kind of time you'll do for this? Drop the weapon, and let's talk about it. Seriously, we'll work something out. Better than going inside for aggravated assault or worse."

Steve shook his head. "Not this time, Detective. I ain't never goin' back inside. Stay where you are, or you'll have a dead lady on your hands."

Wallace had reached the double doors that led to the outside. He used his back to shove them open, then dragged the woman outside and around the corner.

Jacob lost sight of them as he shot forward, hitting the door just as it was closing. They ran out into the field toward the small river separating the Amy Greg facility from some gray industrial buildings.

Steve held the woman's arm just above the elbow, dragging her along with him. All Jacob could do as he ran after them was try to stay close enough to get a shot off or react fast enough if the woman managed to break free.

Moments later, Wallace slowed down near the river's edge and pushed the woman away from him. The woman dropped and rolled to lie on her back while Wallace rested his hands on his knees and panted heavily.

Jacob had him now.

He closed the gap to about fifteen feet and raised his weapon. The Latino woman was out of breath, gasping wildly on the ground at the base of a large tree that overlooked the river. Out of breath and no doubt afraid, she still edged away from Wallace.

"Give it up," Jacob shouted. "Get down on the ground with your hands on your head."

Steven Wallace didn't move. He remained bent over a few feet from the river's edge, still panting like he'd run several miles.

"Where you gonna go now, eh Steve?" Jacob yelled. "Into the river? It's too deep, and the current too swift. You'll drown." He paused to catch his breath. "Drop the weapon and get down on the ground before I put you down."

Steve stood to his full height and glared at Jacob. Tears streamed down Wallace's face.

"What I got to live for, huh?" He gestured wildly toward the facility behind Jacob. "This is my future?" Wallace shook his head. "My life is over, mate. I made some bad choices. I'm through. Just shoot me and get it over with, or I'll jump in the river and take my chances."

"Get on the ground—" Jacob yelled, even though he was tempted to just shoot the bastard.

"I ain't getting down, you piece of shit. Just shoot me."

Wallace raised the weapon and took a step toward Jacob.

Jacob brought his gun up to aim at Wallace's face.

"Drop it! Now!"

Something moved near his feet. The ground shook like the stirrings of an earthquake, and then river water erupted behind Wallace. A nanosecond later, the air vibrated around him like a shock wave punched into his entire body.

Before he was airborne, Jacob caught a glimpse of the Latino woman smacking into the tree. She had been trying to get to her feet and was thrust into the tree by whatever force was shoving Jacob backward.

His consciousness wavered as he landed on the ground.

Just before his eyes shut and his brain turned off, his last sight was of all the windows of the Amy Greg facility blowing out and smashing to pieces in a gigantic explosion of flying glass.

Then Detective Bryce Jacob lost consciousness.

Chapter 12

CHILDREN WERE PLAYING. SOMEONE LAUGHED. BRYCE Jacob angled his head toward the sounds and saw a Frisbee float past him about four feet away.

The sun was shining, the air crisp, the grass green. A German shepherd ran by chasing the Frisbee.

This can't be real. No way this is real.

The air seemed thick, congested. He breathed in and held it as he turned to the right.

Lance Jacob, his son, stood there in his white T-shirt and shorts. The sun bounced off his golden blond hair, glinting off his eyes, warming his smile.

"Come on, Dad," Lance yelled. "Throw it back harder. I want to challenge that dog." His son laughed, bending at the waist.

Two girls were walking their dog off the leash, and now he was trying to catch the Frisbee, and everyone was laughing so much. Lance was happy at the German shepherd's antics, which warmed Jacob's heart.

Jacob retrieved the Frisbee, and after a careful wrap inside his body, he flicked his wrist just right and sent the Frisbee flying toward Lance with the German shepherd tracking it, chasing it.

How could his son be back? How was it possible? Even though there was no rational explanation, Jacob was willing to accept it without question. He *felt* his son's presence more than the truth before his eyes or ears.

The air vibrated, making him scan the immediate area, but everything was normal. Then, everything vibrated again. Pain flared in his head, more specifically, his ears. He watched Lance chase the Frisbee as he raised his hands to his ears. Both hands came away with blood on them.

What the hell? Why are my ears bleeding?

An engine revved somewhere behind him. The air did its weird shake again. Jacob looked up in time to see the breeze had taken the Frisbee, and it was now soaring over Lance's head as he turned and gave chase.

Jacob saw the Camaro and heard the driver revving the engine. He was close enough to see two male occupants in the front seat watching him. They both looked away and watched Lance running.

Jacob started moving, his internal radar pinging even as the air vibrated in its weird way again.

Jacob ran toward Lance, yelling for him to stop. The Frisbee was falling, but it had just crossed the two-foot barrier where the park's grass ended, and the pavement of the road began.

Lance hit the barrier without seeing it, as his attention

was on the flying disk.

The Camaro revved once more.

Jacob watched the back wheels spin as it thrust forward with enormous power, the friction with the concrete causing a shriek.

Over thirty feet back, Jacob was helpless. Lance tripped over the barrier and fell hard onto the surface of the road, his forward motion propelling him sideways where he tucked and rolled like he'd done many times on the soccer field.

The Camaro was too close now.

Jacob was fifteen feet away. He stared at the car as it bore down on his son. The passenger stared back, the driver intent on his goal.

As Jacob made it to the barrier, shouting his son's name, Lance was in a push-up position, about to collect himself and stand. He brought a knee up under his body and stopped to look at his screaming father.

The Camaro's noise drew Lance's attention away from his father.

The air shook again. Jacob's head pounded.

Then he watched, helpless, as the car hit his son and turned him into a flying mass of flesh and blood, all broken and twisted. Contact with the vehicle robbed Lance of his scream of terror, the last sound he'd make on this planet.

The driver glared at Jacob as he passed him, gunning the engine even harder as he raced away from the scene, intent on escape.

When Jacob made it to his son's body, there was nothing he could do, nothing anyone could do. Lance's arms and legs are scattered like God made a mistake. There was no way any life was left in the body of the boy in front of him, not the way his neck was twisted, his skull split open.

But this had been his son. This was his baby boy. How could something like this happen?

Jacob dropped to his knees, his world shattered. The movement on his son's face caught Jacob's attention. He bent down, offering words of comfort, but he knew they held no weight. Lance's eyes fluttered, opened briefly, then his son's eyes shut, and the boy lay still.

Jacob screamed. Then he screamed some more. He shouted at the injustice, the unfairness. But most of all, he screamed because he would never be the same again on the inside. He had lost his son right in front of his own eyes. His baby boy was now on the street before him, lifeless.

Someone shook him.

He opened his eyes and then quickly shut them. He was panting, trying to catch his breath. He was in a bright room. His ex-partner and life-long friend, Everton Charles, stood off to the side as a stranger in a white cloak examined him.

Jacob had woken up in a hospital room. His head pounded, and his throat ached. The doctor stepped back. Jacob motioned at his throat and mouth. He used a straw to ease water down his parched throat a moment later.

It was just a dream, one of many, he told himself. Lance died a year ago. *Cope, Bryce Jacob, you gotta cope. Come back to earth. Relax.*

The doctor spoke, but all Jacob could see was the doctor's mouth moving.

Why can't I hear?

He gingerly felt around his ear. They were both covered

in bandages. He studied Everton's face, then looked at the doctor with the question on his face: *what's going on?*

With his index finger, the doctor motioned to wait a moment and left the room. The worried look on Evers's face didn't concern him. Evers always worried about everything. Jacob was strong. He'd get through whatever happened. If he didn't make it, he'd be with his son. He knew he wasn't suicidal, but when his day came to leave this place, he'd embrace death with open arms and wake to be with Lance.

He looked back at the door so he wouldn't be startled when the doctor appeared before him. The not hearing thing could be worrisome. He wondered to what extent his ears were damaged.

Someone moved past the door.

Jacob jolted upright, flaring his headache. Evers was on him instantly, easing him back into the bed. Jacob spun to look at him and could tell he was asking what was wrong.

Jacob eased back down and pointed at the door. He mouthed, *did you see who that was? The boy who walked by the door could've been Lance's twin.*

The doctor re-entered the room with a pad of paper and a couple of pens. He stopped at the bed and began writing. Jacob touched the doctor's waist and moved him to the side so he could watch the door. The doctor frowned at the gesture, appearing confused but moved, nonetheless.

When the doctor finished writing, he turned the pad toward Jacob.

Jacob read what he'd written. "You've been here almost a week. Your hearing will return. We suspect there's no permanent damage. Both ears bled for two days. We have ointment and gauze in there until tomorrow. An unknown source knocked you out. The media have called it an "Air Quake," whatever that means. Experts are saying it was something akin to a shock wave. It vibrates your body and your brain, causing the week-long coma, but nothing else seems amiss. If you feel up to it, you should be ready to leave the hospital by tomorrow."

Jacob met the doctor's gaze, nodded his understanding, and stared at the door. A nurse walked by.

Someone placed the pen in his hand. He turned back to the doctor and his friend. It was his turn to write something.

"Why doesn't anyone know what caused the Air Quake? What happened to the woman and Steven Wallace? They were both out there with me."

He handed the pad to Everton, then watched as Evers read it and wrote his answer. Jacob took the pad back.

"No idea on the cause yet. The woman's name is Maria Lopez. Both she and Steven Wallace are still in comas in this hospital."

Jacob met Evers's gaze, nodded, and laid back his head. After a moment, he shifted his gaze to stare at the door again. The pad was taken from him. Then, Evers walked around to block his vision of the door. He thrust the pad down for Jacob to read it.

"What's up with the door? Waiting for someone?"

Jacob took the pen. "A kid walked by dressed in a white T-shirt and shorts. He had something yellow in his hand. It looked like a Frisbee. I could've sworn it was Lance."

Everton read this, then turned to the doctor and spoke to him. The doctor glanced at Jacob and back to Everton. They talked more, and then the doctor wrote on the pad.

"Get some rest, Bryce. I'll come back to check on you later."

Jacob nodded and shut his eyes. When he opened them a few minutes later, his friend sat in a chair on the other side of the private room, flipping through a magazine.

Jacob turned his attention to the open hospital room door.

He lay there staring at it, hoping for another glimpse of his son.

It was impossible, as Lance had been dead for a year, but something told him it was his boy.

The Frisbee was one thing.

But Bryce saw the glint in the boy's eye, the smile on his face.

It was Lance's smile—one hundred percent.

Chapter 13

A CONSTANT BUZZING, DRONING SOUND INTRUDED on her consciousness.

Maria Lopez fought through the pain in her head and opened her eyes to a dimly lit hospital room. No one waited for her. There were no flowers. With most of her family still in South America, they wouldn't even know she was in the hospital.

A woman sat on the bed to her right, catching Maria's eye. The woman eased to the edge of the mattress, then smiled at Maria, nodding once.

"Good morning," she whispered. "Isn't it going to be a beautiful day?"

Maria nodded to be polite, even though her head throbbed. "I'm sure it will be."

"I'm Julie Grennick. It's nice to meet you." The woman hopped off the edge of the bed and moved toward the door. "But now I must be going."

"Can you tell me how long I've been here?" Maria asked.

"Just over a week, I think. I've been here a while longer, but I'm checking myself out now. I'm all healed, done with this visit."

The woman seemed to be acting strange. From where Maria lay in her bed, she couldn't see the woman's feet, and her nightgown was so long that Maria couldn't see the woman's legs moving. Yet, as the woman approached the door to leave, it almost appeared as if she *glided* there as her legs didn't seem to move.

"What were you in the hospital for? What healed?" Maria winced at the pain caused by speaking. She closed her eyes a moment, touching her temple.

When she opened her eyes again, the old woman had stopped near the door and turned back to face her.

"I entered the hospital with severe headaches. After a round of tests, the doctors told me I had an inoperable brain tumor. They gave me a month to live, maybe even weeks, but I haven't felt this good in a long time. Now, I must be going. Take care of yourself, Maria Lopez."

The woman spun around and drifted out the door.

When did I say my name?

Inoperable brain tumor? That was something serious. It could stop a person in their tracks, change their life—what little was left of it—forever, yet this woman was spry and jovial. Well, good for her.

Maria closed her eyes and rested.

Something bumped her bed. She opened them again.

At least four people dressed in hospital scrubs had entered the room. The lights had been turned on. Maria saw them shouting something at each other. It appeared they were quite frantic about something and addressing the empty bed beside her.

Maria turned to look at Julie's bed and then jumped back, her eyes widening despite the pain in her head.

Julie Grennick was back in her bed and looked pale—snow-white pale. Maybe something happened to her on the way out of the hospital.

A doctor was pumping her chest. It certainly appeared worse than moments before. What could have happened to her? They were acting as if Julie was dead.

A nurse was reading a monitor. Another nurse was offering the doctor some kind of instrument.

In minutes, it was all over. The doctor moved his mouth, but Maria couldn't hear what he said. Then he lifted the covers over Julie's face, and they wheeled her bed out of the room.

One nurse stayed behind. She filled a glass with water, dropped a bendable straw into it, and moved to Maria's bedside. She drank on it heartily as her throat was dry.

The nurse grabbed a small piece of paper and started writing something on it. Within minutes, Maria had learned how she came to be in the hospital, how long she had been there, and why she wasn't able to hear yet, even though she'd be able to leave tomorrow.

The nurse touched a piece of the medical tape that covered Maria's right ear. The edge came away easily. She pulled, and Maria felt a small tug on the inside of her ear like a Q-Tip had been caught. Then, the nurse withdrew the bandage. A small amount of blood had crusted up on the innermost part of the gauze.

Although not as clear, her hearing had returned to a small degree.

Maria asked how Mrs. Grennick was doing. It didn't look good moments ago. She explained how they had spoken to one another about ten minutes before, and Mrs. Grennick seemed so happy and light that she'd healed and was leaving the hospital. Julie had glided across the room and went through the door, saying something about checking herself out of the hospital.

The nurse stared at Maria for a long moment. She stood at the foot of Maria's bed and used her fingers to cross her chest, evidently a religious woman.

Then she turned and stormed out of the room in a hurry.

Maria frowned. What the hell was that about? Why is everybody so weird in this hospital?

She would check out tomorrow and not look back. Whatever hit them out by that river probably saved her life as that madman had a knife. She shuddered at the memory of being taken and pushed to run with the threat of that knife-like weapon in the guy's hand.

Luck brought that handsome cop to her rescue. She remembered being surprised when they got to the river and turned around to see a man had chased them, and he had a gun trained on the guy with the knife.

It all ended so quickly after that. Something shook them off their feet. She seemed to remember hitting the tree and falling, only to wake here.

A week in a coma? That's what the nurse said. How could that be possible?

The door opened. A woman walked in, her face red and wet with tears.

She moved without purpose toward Julie's empty bed.

"Did you get a chance to meet my mother?" the woman asked.

Maria put it together rather quickly. "Yes—" Her throat cracked. She swallowed and tried again. "Yes, we spoke a little while ago."

The woman looked to be in her thirties. She turned to stare at Maria.

"What did you two talk about?"

The woman's lower lip quivered. She seemed more upset by the second.

Maria's hearing was weirdly lopsided, so she grabbed the bandage on the left ear and pulled it off, too.

"Julie woke up, got off her bed, and walked to the door. She talked about how beautiful the day was going to be and that she had never felt better. She said she came here with inoperable brain cancer but that now she was healed. Then she left. I don't know how she returned to her bed and what happened afterward. They just took her out, I think. I'm sorry. I wish I could help more."

The woman grabbed a tissue from a box by Julie's bed, wiped her face, and then turned away from Maria as her crying intensified.

"My mother died in this room." She gasped a breath. "You couldn't have talked to her."

Maria stared at the tiled ceiling, pressing her head into the pillow. What was going on? How could Julie feel great one second, then be dead the next? Also, was she being called a liar? If so, how did she know the woman's name?

"I'm sorry for your loss," Maria said. "How could I know her name if I'm lying to you? I was in a coma until half an hour ago, so I'm told. I only just woke up myself."

The door opened. The nurse from earlier stuck her head in.

"Did that help?" the nurse asked.

The daughter nodded and walked to the door. She turned back to Maria before leaving.

"Thank you. I'm happy to hear she left feeling better. May God be with you."

The door closed behind her, and Maria was alone again.

What was that? What just happened? She would be mistaken if she thought I spoke to a dead person. I don't talk to dead people—that's ridiculous.

Nevertheless, Maria eased downward, allowing the covers to creep up her neck as she glanced around the room.

Movement caught her eye. She looked toward the window.

Something skirted past it, then disappeared.

What floor is this? How high is my room?

Condensation covered the window like water seeping through a wall, leaving moisture behind.

Someone or something drew in the condensation on the window, but she couldn't see anyone.

She sat upright in bed, ignoring the pain in her head, and stared at the heart drawn in the moisture. It looked exactly like Cupid's heart, complete with the arrow.

In the center were the initials M.L. and J.T., just like her husband did as often as he could when he was alive.

Bathroom mirrors, windows, the sides of trees, and letter magnets on the fridge—wherever he could find, he would jot this reminder of his love for her and the world to see.

Who did this on her hospital room window? Who would be so cruel?

Maria lay back and covered her eyes as she cried. What was happening to her? She needed John now more than ever.

As she lay in her hospital bed, alone now, she kept asking herself, who could have known about John's arrows?

It had been their secret from the world.

Chapter 14

STEVEN WALLACE WOKE UP, SCANNED THE room and the single handcuff on his right arm, then used his left to yank all the bandages off his head. It took longer than expected, but no one entered the room while he frantically undid the gauze.

A needle was stuck in his right arm just below the elbow. He eased it out slowly, then held his thumb over the dot of blood that formed at the needle's exit point.

He studied the room they'd moved him to while he waited for the blood to clot. It made him think they'd transferred him to a hospital rather than leave him at the detox center. At least it was a private room because his was the only bed. The window was dark, and the main light was off, so it was easy to deduce it had to be sometime in the middle of the night. The only glow came from a small nightlight and the light seeping in from under the door. He couldn't hear anything outside the room—a perfect time to leave.

He glanced down at the cuffed arm.

"Shit," he whispered, then frowned.

That was weird. He didn't hear his voice the same. Like his ears were dead.

He rattled the cuff on the metal it attached to but couldn't hear anything.

"Fuck."

Steve scrambled off the bed and found the release switch on the bed's wheels. Then he dragged it away from the wall and started looking for his clothes. He found them in a small closet, but the bed couldn't get close enough, so he had to stretch to reach them. Five minutes later, with great effort, he was dressed in his socks and jeans, but the shirt wouldn't drop over the cuff on his wrist.

That would pose a problem.

He hadn't thought that far ahead. What would he do now? He couldn't run down the street cuffed to a bed.

The bed had to go.

He examined under the railing but could not see a place to unhook it, nor could he slip his arm out of the handcuff.

Cuffed the way he was, unless someone came with a key, the bed had to escape with him. Not only that, they'd probably placed a cop at his door. What if a cop was on the other side of the door guarding his room? He wouldn't be surprised after what he did at the detox center.

He hatched a plan. If the bed had to go with him, he would toss it out the window and make sure he landed on it. Then he could run with it as the bed had large white wheels.

Whatever happened, he had to leave, and if that was his only option, then fuck it.

Two feet from the door sat a small wooden end table with magazines on it. He moved over to it, then shoved it with his foot until it sat in front of the door. After that, he grabbed the other end table and, with great effort, placed it on top of the first one.

That familiar headache was back, but it was more tolerable now.

Certain the weight of the tables would slow anyone who tried to get in his room, he pushed the bed over to the window and looked down.

Height always looked bigger from above. Even though the third-floor window looked high, it really wasn't. His hands shook when he undid the clasp to unlock the window.

How long had he been knocked out? What did they feed him? Could he go through withdrawal symptoms while unconscious?

Things to ponder when he was back on the street.

He unlocked the window and reached for the bottom to lift it up.

Wait, the window was nowhere near the right size to toss out a bed. How would he accomplish that? Break the window and the surrounding frame? If so, he'd have to do it fast. Shove the bed through and jump at the same time. Could he nail it, though, and land just right—

"I wouldn't do that if I were you."

Steve jumped and let out a small yelp. "Who's there?" He ducked and scanned the empty room. "Where are you? I can't see you?"

"I'm over here."

The voice came from the darkened corner. The edge of a

man's face came into view. He looked familiar, but Steve grew impatient, which fueled his anger.

"Do I know you?" Steve asked. "What the fuck you doin' in my private hospital room?"

"This room is hardly private." The man smiled. "The only reason you're alone here is because you're a guarded prisoner. A cop is asleep just outside your door. If you'd like, I could wake him for you."

Steve stepped away from the window. "You threatening me?"

"Not at all."

"Then why wake the cop? Do you want to rat me out? Yo, that's a threat, which makes you a nark."

"A nark? Hardly the case."

"Then what're you doing in my room?"

"I came to warn you."

Steve stepped closer to the man in the corner, dragging the bed with him. He crossed the floor with ease, the bed's wheels rolling quietly.

"What warning? Huh? Another threat?"

"You have a task to complete before you die."

Steve stopped moving. "Die?" He tried to smile to hide his fear, but something about the man's tone shot a spike of anxiety into his gut. The man creeped him out, and his smile drifted off his face.

"Yes, die. You need to help Bryce Jacob with something. I'm unsure of the details, but I know you must do this to save the others. That many people aren't supposed to go so early."

"What the hell you be talking about? Help that pig? No fuckin' way."

"I assure you, I'm not discussing Hell. This is real. This is here, today. Tell Bryce Jacob what I've said and stay close to him. You'll know what to do when the time comes."

"Or I die, is that it?" Steve felt queasy now, his stomach not handling this conversation well. Help a dirty cop or die? What kind of choice was that?

"You'll die anyway," the man whispered. "Better you do it with honor."

"Sticking to the threats, eh?" Steve moved closer.

The door was blocked. The man couldn't run for help, nor could anyone get into the room too fast. Steve could literally drop the guy with one arm tied behind his back. This was going to be easy.

"Remember to contact Jacob—"

Steve rushed him, his free arm up and flailing, and his head lowered, the bed coming in behind him. Pain shot up his handcuffed wrist, but he ignored it because this man needed to learn a lesson. Nobody threatened his life and walked away without at least a few bruises.

His forehead connected with the wall, then his shoulder. Pain flared, sharp, and hot. He grunted and dropped to the floor. How did he miss? He'd been one foot away.

Right arm raised to the side of the bed, Wallace glanced around the room. It was empty. He was on the floor of his hospital room, all alone.

Someone knocked on the door.

"Hey, let us in," someone shouted from the other side of the door.

Steve brought his legs up to his chest and wrapped his free arm around himself. Who had he been talking to? Where did the man go? That had to be the most vivid hallucination he'd ever had, and yet there weren't any narcotics in his system. Unless there really was someone standing in the darkened corner.

The knocking on the door increased, and the shouting from the hallway continued. Then the door moved inward as someone banged into it.

Could he be losing his mind?

Both legs bounced with a nervous tick, and his hands shook uncontrollably. What was that shit about death, and when was it coming?

Since there was no one in the room and it wasn't a hallucination, he had to have been talking to the Grim Reaper. There was no such thing as ghosts and heaven, at least not in Steve's world.

Or was that someone from up above?

His hospital door smashed open.

Several people barged in and turned on the lights. They shouted at him, but he paid them no attention.

If he had a soul to save, and that was an angel coming down to offer him an option, then maybe he would take it.

When they heaved him up off the floor and laid him back on the bed, his thoughts came back to Detective Bryce Jacob.

And he realized he would never help that man unless Detective Jacob wanted an ass-kicking. Then maybe he would lend a hand.

Chapter 15

Bryce Jacob sat up and finished eating the dreary hospital food as the morning sun pierced the curtains in the window of his room.

"Look, I'm telling you," he said between bites. "I thought I saw Lance."

"I hear you, but we both know that isn't possible." Evers stared at him for a moment. "Also, don't let the sarge or anyone else hear you say you're seeing your dead son. They'll take your badge and gun, my friend." Evers moved closer. "Do you want to talk about your dreams?"

"What dreams?" Jacob shoved the elevated tray away from the bedside with his plastic food holders. Most of his hearing had returned, but it was accompanied by a loud ringing, something the doctor said was tinnitus. Apparently, it would dissipate over the next few weeks.

"I spent quite a few nights here with you. A few times, you called out your son's name. The night before you woke from the coma, you thrashed around in bed and screamed his name. How have you been handling that for a year?"

Jacob laid his head on the pillow, adjusting the bed to recline back with the controls on the side.

"Handling it? More like I haven't been handling it."

The past year had been a living horror. It was like a piece of him died in that park, and now it was eating him alive. Insomnia had come in the long, lonely nights—except for when he took a Xanax—but he kept it to himself. Otherwise, they'd have never let him come back to work to search for his son's murderers.

"Look, Evers, I need to find my son's killers before I can allow myself any kind of normal life again. Lance deserves some justice, and the guys on homicide are holding their dicks. So, of course, I will dream about my son as he's in every waking thought, too."

"Word at HQ last week was McGregor wanted to suspend you. Did he?"

"No, he warned me hardcore, though. Told me to back off and do my job. I'm supposed to take a break, or he'll send me on a vacation or something—"

Jacob stopped talking. Something he remembered brought him back to the meeting with his sergeant.

"What? What is it?" Everton asked.

"I just remembered. McGregor was hiding something."

"Hiding something? What are you talking about? Sergeants hide everything all the time. What else is new?"

"When we were having our meeting, Spencer from homicide interrupted us to update him on a kidnapping— some scientist and his wife. The guy worked on sound waves or shock waves or some shit. Anyway, McGregor asked Spencer if the kidnappers were interested in this scientist if they were building a bomb." He glanced at Evers, who was staring at him intensely. "What just happened by the river? Wasn't it a shockwave that hit us?"

"You're reaching here."

"No, I'm not. McGregor said that if I didn't watch myself, I, too, would be a casualty."

"You know as well as I do that he meant you'd lose your job." Evers guffawed. "Like the sergeant would threaten you."

Jacob watched his friend and truly saw him. Evers stood by him when Lance was killed and buried. He was there when Bryce's wife left. Evers was his friend from the police academy. The man before him was like a brother, yet he didn't see the Everton he knew. He saw a broken man, wounded by life and not willing to see, to really see what Bryce saw. For the first time since Lance died, everything became clear. He knew what he had to do going forward.

"Everton, something's wrong with McGregor. I've felt it for a long time. We both know cops go rogue sometimes. The temptation is too great on some arrests. Who's to say a sergeant wouldn't be on the take? And if he knows about this shockwave bomb and he sent me out to that detox center, then how do I know if he sent me out there to get me killed?"

Evers walked away from the edge of Jacob's bed and opened the door to the hospital room. After glancing out into the hallway, he turned back, closed the door, and glared at Bryce.

"That is a serious allegation. I'm going to pretend I

didn't hear it. While pretending I didn't hear what you just said, I'm going down to the cafeteria to get a coffee and a newspaper. When I come back, we'll talk about getting you out of this place." Evers stared a moment longer, then nodded at Bryce. "Perhaps the sarge was right. You should go to Hawaii and sit on a beach, or better yet, head to Greece or some shit. You need to chill the fuck out, my friend."

Jacob watched the door shut behind Evers. He knew what he was thinking was right. As soon as he'd returned to work after Lance had died, McGregor had reassigned him from the case he'd been working on. Gave him some bullshit reason about stress and how it was too hard to chase the drug manufacturers while dealing with grief.

The case he'd worked the week before his bereavement leave had led him to a company called Giotech Pharmaceuticals. He left the report on McGregor's desk that fateful Friday evening, then took Lance to the park on the Saturday to play Frisbee. After his leave for bereavement, McGregor told him that Giotech had been investigated, and they were clean. The case was closed. Bad leads, bad informants.

Bryce had worked case after case, brought on criminal informants, and made arrests up the chain to a totally legit company.

But were they? Could it be possible Giotech had a side division making and producing narcotics for the street?

What if that wasn't the case, and Bryce had it all wrong?

He sat up in bed, his mind working over the details. He suddenly wanted out of the hospital. Perhaps a visit to Giotech was his next stop.

Sitting on the bed's edge, he noticed a woman in his room.

He jumped as her sudden appearance startled him. What the hell was she wearing, and where did she come from?

"Who are you?" he asked.

She leaned forward but remained in the shadows. He had an eerie feeling about her. Jacob didn't spook easily, but this woman had an eerie glow about her. Her long dress appeared to have soft lights behind it, illuminating it from the inside. It was almost like she had taken small Christmas tree lights and strung them under the fabric of her dress.

"My name is Ulea. I have come to talk to you."

Jacob slid off the edge of the bed and tested his legs. The nurses had been exercising his legs while he was in the coma, but they were still tentative to walk on. With one hand on the bed, he knew he wouldn't be moving too fast today. He turned back to her.

"Talk to me?" he said, his tone gruff. "About what? McGregor?"

"You need to listen to a woman named Kramer Kay. She will call you."

"Who the hell's Kramer Kay? What kind of name is that, and why will she call me?"

"She will help you to understand what's happening to you. Also, Lance will be there, so try not to be startled."

Will Lance be there? What the fuck?

"Who put you up to this? This some kind of sick joke?" Jacob panted as standing became an effort. Or was he panting because of the strange woman and what she'd said?

An announcement in the hallway asked for a doctor to

come to room 404, drawing his attention.

Why am I so connected to what is happening around me?

"You will understand everything in a short time. You wrote this in your blueprint before coming here. This is your time to shine. You are the strong one of the three. It affected you the most. Find Kramer Kay and stay away from McGregor. He's on his way here. You mustn't see him."

"What the hell are you talking about—"

The door opened suddenly. Jacob jerked his head toward the door and saw Everton run in.

"Hey, Evers, get a load of this woman." He pointed at the woman in the corner.

The corner was empty.

"Get a load of what woman?" Evers asked. "And how come you're standing on your own? You shouldn't do that so early without someone to help support you."

Shock settled over his system, and he almost fell. He would've face-planted if he didn't have a strong grip on the railing. Was he seeing things? First, it was Lance in the hallway, then a strange woman in the corner of his hospital room.

"She was right there," he said weakly, pointing into the corner. "She talked about me writing something in my blueprint and how—shit!"

"It's okay, man." Everton moved closer. "Seriously, you have to calm down. You're scaring me."

Jacob leaned back on the edge of the bed as his legs were about to give out. He twisted around to study the room, but no one was hiding anywhere. The woman had disappeared.

"A woman was just here," he said again. "She told me to

talk to Kramer Kay and not to see the sarge—"

"Okay, Jacob. That's enough." Everton moved to within a foot of his face. "You can't talk like that and expect your life to return to normal. What would McGregor think listening to you now?"

"I was told to avoid him."

"For obvious reasons."

"No, seriously. I was warned. He's coming to see me here, at the hospital. I was told to stay away from him. Why do you think that is?"

Evers stepped away to pace at the end of the bed.

"Jacob, how did you know he was coming?"

"I just told you. I was informed by some woman who just fucking disappeared into thin air. I know how that sounds. I'm not an idiot." His voice rose. "I saw her with my own eyes and heard her with my ears. I trust my senses. They haven't lied to me before. She even said Lance would be there at some meeting or something."

Jacob lay back on the bed.

Everton stopped pacing. "This is fucked. I feel like I lost a friend. You need help, buddy."

"You haven't lost me, asshole. I'm still your friend. Something weird is happening, and I need your help to sort it out. What I don't need is your judgment. Just accept the shit, and let's work it out."

"Maybe, but right now, I'm going to leave to try to digest what's happening to you. In the meantime, I'd advise you don't talk about this shit with anyone. Seriously, if I think you've lost your mind, then anyone else listening to this will have you committed."

Everton strode for the door and slipped into the hallway without another word. The door closed silently behind him.

Jacob stared at the corner of the room where the woman had spoken to him. If his own boss wanted to remove him and he was sent to the Amy Greg facility to be killed, then McGregor would want to finish the job. If that were the case, then Jacob needed to find out why and how it was connected to Lance.

Something told him it was all connected to Lance.

For some reason, his mind had an intense clarity.

He could see everything so much better as every hour passed.

Chapter 16

Bill McGregor ended his call and slipped his cell phone into his pocket. He had just called the station to have Everton Charles ordered back for some bogus paperwork filing dispute. He sat in the hospital's underground parking lot, staring at Everton's cruiser, waiting for him to jump in and drive from the hospital.

No one suspected him, and no one ever would. The job was almost done. Less than a week from now, he would be on a plane and gone from American soil forever.

The access door to the elevator opened. Everton emerged and walked across the lot toward his car. McGregor waited until he was in and driving out before he stepped from his department-issued cruiser.

As soon as he locked the door, his cell rang again. He looked at call display.

"Shit."

He pressed the answer button. "Yeah?"

"Are you at the hospital?"

"Yes."

"Good. Do you anticipate any problems?"

The man's accent always bothered him because it reminded him of their true purpose. McGregor didn't care about the true purpose of any of what they were doing. His only purpose was cash.

"There won't be any problems."

"Good. Contact us when you're finished, and don't fuck this up."

McGregor ended the call, turned the phone to vibrate, and slipped it into his pocket. The warning to not make a mistake was rare, but he understood it because they'd tried to take out Bryce Jacob before and missed.

McGregor entered the hospital and took the elevator to the main floor, where he purchased flowers at the gift shop. When he reached the fifth floor, a nurse directed him to Jacob's room.

He took a deep breath and opened the door.

The room was empty.

Water was running in the bathroom. Light emanated from under the door.

"Jacob?" He called.

McGregor set the flowers on the side table and pulled out the syringe he had prepared. He took the plastic cap off the end and stepped to the bathroom door, his head against it.

"Jacob?"

Someone grabbed him from behind, and the needle was knocked from his hand. He struggled to remain upright, but the arm around his throat was locked solid, stealing his breath and dragging him up and backward.

"What the fuck!"

McGregor recognized Jacob's voice close to his ear.

Equilibrium lost, they both tumbled back and hit the floor. McGregor made sure to have all his weight land on Jacob, hoping to knock the wind out of him or at least dislodge the arm around his throat.

For a brief moment, the arm moved away. It was only enough to catch a short breath, but then the hammer hold retightened.

Jacob meant to kill him. He understood that now.

His vision clouded over while his lungs protested as they fought for air. His hands weakened, and he started to give up.

When he thought it was over and the room dimmed in his vision around the edges, the door to the hospital room burst open. Everton rushed in and dove on them, wrestling Jacob off McGregor's throat.

Air shot into his lungs, and the world came back into focus. He moved away from Jacob and Everton to lean against the wall and try to breathe again.

"What the fuck are you doing?" Everton shouted at Bryce. "You could've killed him. Look at him in the corner there all red and gasping for breath and shit. What were you thinking, numbnuts?"

Jacob leaned up against the base of the bed. "He came here to kill me," he panted, seemingly out of breath, too. "He came to finish the job." He glared at McGregor, then continued. "That's why he sent me to the detox facility that day."

McGregor's lungs were working better now. He was

breathing better, but his throat felt compressed and swollen.

McGregor saw the moment Everton took in the needle on the floor.

"What's in the needle, Sarge?"

"I have no idea." He inhaled, then exhaled, his throat raw. "Jacob pulled it on me when I walked in here. I brought him flowers, and he went nuts."

Jacob started to get up. Once on both legs, he turned and ran at McGregor, landing on him before Everton could react.

"Did you kill Lance, too, you bastard?" Jacob shouted. "How are you connected to it all?"

Jacob landed punch after punch. McGregor didn't know how much more he could take. In his weakened state, he had almost no defense. As fast as the assault began, though, it stopped when Everton pulled Jacob off him again.

"Jacob, seriously," Everton screamed. "You want to end up in jail? What the fuck, man?"

The door opened, and a nurse stuck her head in.

Everton turned to her. "Get out. We're having a private meeting."

To her credit, the nurse pulled her head back out and shut the door without delay.

"Jacob," Everton said. "Can I get you to agree to stop attacking the sarge for a second? Fuck, man!"

Jacob nodded, his face red and out of breath.

"Okay, good."

McGregor tasted blood on his tongue. Jacob landed half a dozen punches, and one must've split his lip.

"McGregor's rogue," Jacob spouted. "He's hooked up with some Russians."

"Russians?" Everton gasped. "Now I know you've lost your mind. Where are you getting information like that?"

"I just know. I put it all together."

Everton stepped between them. "Explain this to me. Let's get it all out before the sarge calls this in and has you arrested."

"Before Lance was killed," Jacob continued, "I was working a case that led me to a major shipment of meth. I can't remember how McGregor knew about it before me, but he did. Without going through all the details, I discovered the shipping containers were owned by several companies, eventually leading me back to Giotech Pharmaceuticals. When I checked them out, they were owned by Americans with Russian connections in high places. I researched as much as possible and put it all on McGregor's desk. The next day, they were watching me. Then they ran over Lance and killed him. The sarge here was probably told to finish the job."

"Jacob, are you serious? Is that how you want to end your career? Accusing our boss of working with the Russians and murder?" Everton raised his voice. "Have you lost your fucking mind?"

Everton turned away from McGregor and knelt in front of Jacob.

McGregor watched as Everton laid into Detective Jacob.

"Dude, I'm sorry, but until you're feeling better, you're forcing me to commit you involuntarily. There's no other choice here. You've lost all sense of judgment."

McGregor eased the gun out of his shoulder holster. He didn't have a sound suppressor on it as he didn't think he'd have to use the gun in the hospital, but he could see no other way now. For him to walk out of this hospital and keep breathing, Detective Bryce Jacob had to be killed.

McGregor took careful aim, then fired the weapon.

The sound was deafening in the confined room.

Everton slumped down onto one knee, then fell in front of Jacob as he tried to turn around and look at McGregor.

The bullet had entered Everton's back high up. It would've exited through his pectoral muscle, doing enough damage in his chest to end the man's life. Even though they were surrounded by life-saving equipment, nothing could mend what had happened to Everton's chest.

The wounded man scrunched up into a ball and moaned loudly.

Bryce Jacob seemed to be having a hard time getting to his feet.

"Ten days off your legs can be a bitch, eh?" McGregor laughed.

He lifted the weapon to aim at Jacob's face. He applied pressure to the trigger, and when there was a loud report, something punched his chest.

He lowered his weapon and stared at it. Did it fire backward?

What the hell happened?

Then he got punched again.

Open wounds and small circular holes had formed on his chest. His gun arm dropped, the weapon falling from his grip. He reached for his wound to try to keep the blood in.

"What happened?" he whispered out loud, his voice weakened by the chest injury.

When he glanced up, it all became clear.

Everton hadn't scrunched into a ball because of the pain. He had rolled into himself to reach a gun in an ankle holster. A small caliber weapon dangled from his hand as he stared at Bill, probably waiting to see if he needed to shoot him again.

Jacob had gotten to his feet, his face contorted in pain and anguish as he stumbled to the door. Then he yanked it open and shouted into the corridor for a doctor.

It was too late for McGregor, though. Blood dribbled past his lips now. Breathing in and out became a chore as at least one lung filled with blood.

He shut his eyes and whispered a little prayer under his breath. Faith had been elusive during his life. Maybe now was a good time to believe there was something of an afterlife.

On his last breath, he opened his eyes, and the room faded.

As if pushed, he felt himself released from his body. The feeling was intense and liberating as he was now weightless. He floated around the room, surveying the carnage. He got the impression that Everton would live. His wounds weren't fatal after all.

When he angled higher and was about to leave the room, something caught his eye, making him look back.

Jacob was staring at him, wide-eyed.

McGregor floated a moment, their eyes locked on each other. Then he glided to the door, and Jacob said something about everything being okay. He got what he needed, and he'd see him soon.

Whatever that meant.

The one-sided conversation was too weird for McGregor to care about as he ascended elsewhere, leaving the issues of another life behind as he moved on to the next one.

Chapter 17

"WHAT THE FUCK ARE YOU TALKING about? Someone, please tell me why Bryce Jacob isn't dead?"

Boris Ivanov got up from his chair, showing off his considerable size at six foot, four inches. Both men standing before him shrunk back a step.

"I'm sorry, sir. I have no idea how this could happen. McGregor had specific instructions. He knew failure wasn't an option. My source confirms McGregor is dead, though."

"How is that possible?" Boris's voice rose along with his anger. "Did they allow Jacob to carry a weapon in his coma?" He stepped around his desk and removed his tweed jacket, then tossed it across the papers and folders scattered atop the desk. He moved swiftly between the two men, heading for the door. "Take me to Mr. Morgan. It is time for him to earn his life."

Both men dutifully followed him. He led them through the corridors of the fourth-floor office wing of Giotech

Pharmaceuticals without saying another word. They took the elevator into the basement, where only a few scientists worked. In total, six people knew of the existence of Operation Cuba, and in less than a week after the operation, there would only be one person left alive—him—to travel home and take the credit.

"Has he eaten today?" Boris asked.

"No. He still refuses to eat until we bring his wife to him."

"Is he conscious?"

"Last we checked, yes, he was. That was an hour ago."

Boris rolled up his sleeves as he entered the men's sleeping quarters. At the end of the hallway were the two jail cell-like rooms that he had built in case anyone working on Operation Cuba had decided to stop. Prison for a day or two without rations to organize their priorities seemed to work on the softer men of today. The Gulag was something altogether different. Today's man was much weaker and easier to conform to. Don't feed them for two days, and they'll kill their brother for a steak.

Otherwise, a nine-millimeter bullet for one of the men often changed the attitude of the rest of them.

"Open this door," he instructed Viktor Miklos, his partner on the project. Both men had known each other since their early days in the homeland, and they were both called into action on the same day to lead this operation just over two years ago.

Viktor punched a code on the illuminated keypad, and a small chime announced the door was unlocked. Boris opened the door and stepped into the gloom.

Dan Morgan sat on the bench near the back.

"Where's my wife?" Morgan asked.

"Of course," Boris said as he walked over to Dan. "Your wife."

He grabbed Morgan's hair with his left hand, arched his face back, and brought his right fist down onto Morgan's cheek like the fall of a hammer. Morgan's skin split, and he crumpled to the floor, blood oozing from the wound.

"Get him up," Boris shouted.

Anger rose in him, clouding his thoughts. He hated everything American. He'd been here too long, waiting for the call to duty. Two years ago, when the call came, he felt useful again, like his mother now cared for her lost son. With less than a week left in Operation Cuba, he couldn't allow mistakes—or slow production due to ineptitude to ruin their chances of success.

"Bring him to the operation room. I want everyone to watch this. There will be no more dissent, no more dictating terms to us, and no more mistakes."

Boris turned and left, followed by his two men, who dragged the moaning scientist, Dan Morgan, between them.

Boris reached the operation room, grabbed a chair, and placed it in the center so all six men could see from their stations.

"Bring him here."

Morgan was placed on the chair. Boris grabbed the man's hair again, yanking his face up to look at him.

"Oh, that looks bad." He glanced at Viktor. "Go get me the first aid kit and a pair of scissors."

That's what he loved about Viktor. Even when asking for

something odd like scissors, he just did it. No questions, no wonderment on his face, only the fulfillment of his duty to a superior officer.

Boris released Morgan's hair and stepped back.

"We have an issue that we haven't figured out. This is why you're here. We need your help. We offered you money. You didn't want it. We offered you freedom, and all you kept asking for was your wife. She is in another holding cell. She is of no use to us. So I have decided to give you your wife."

"I won't help you to kill people," Morgan whispered.

"You Americans make me sick," Boris shouted. "So patriotic, and yet so stupid. Are you blind, Mr. Morgan? Do you not understand what this is, who we are? You're a smart man. I'm sure you can figure it out."

Viktor returned and stuck out his hand with the first aid kit and scissors in it. Boris waved it off.

"Take the gauze from the first aid kit, bandages, and duct tape with you. Use those scissors to do the cutting."

Viktor looked down at the objects in his hand. "What do you want me to cut?"

"Mr. Morgan here wants his wife before he will agree to work with us. So, bring him his wife. Piece by piece. I want the ring finger first."

"*No*," Morgan shouted and made to stand.

Boris shoved him back down. "Stay in that chair, or I will cut out your eyes, Mr. Morgan."

"Okay, okay, I will help you." Morgan was reduced to tears. "Tell me what you want. I'll do it. Just leave my wife alone."

Boris shook his head. "Too late. How do you Americans

say it? Something about the horse being gone and the gate is open. You should've shut the gate when you had the chance, Mr. Morgan. You should have shut the gate." Boris tsked tsked, shaking his head.

He looked up at Viktor. "Bring me her finger."

Viktor walked away and disappeared down the hallway without hesitation.

"No, please. I was mistaken. I didn't know how serious you were. Please, listen to me …"

"I believe you will help us, Mr. Morgan," Boris nodded. "I am a master of persuasion. I will keep your lovely wife alive as long as I can to ensure your assistance doesn't waver. Then, when this is over, you and your wife will be free to leave."

Morgan crumpled into sobs, his chest wracked by heaves. Boris watched this with growing disdain. War was Hell. He knew that growing up with a father in the KGB, he learned firsthand what war was.

Now, the Americans would pay a small price.

He glanced around the large underground control room. "Have I got everyone's attention? We are on a timetable. Next Saturday, we are all scheduled to fly home as long as everything happens on schedule. If it doesn't, and we fly home, we are flying to our executions. Have no illusion. Finish Operation Cuba, or die."

He prided himself in his ability to motivate his people. Just like his father taught him. Brute strength and an iron fist worked every time. He was able to *make* people listen. He never wavered, never blinked, and ruled through the use of fear. After all, wasn't that how religion worked? By using fear of Hell and guilt to avoid sin? Today, Boris was conducting a sermon. This was his church.

A woman screamed from the back hallway.

Morgan's wife's finger was being cut off.

"Do you hear that?" Boris asked, a smile playing across his lips.

Morgan was still crying on the chair like a baby. He looked up at Boris, his eyes bloodshot. "Why? Why us? Why did you pick me?"

"I told you on the way to this facility. I need your expertise with shockwaves. Since my experiment in the river wasn't a complete success, I need you to correct our mistakes."

"I'm a teacher at the Fraser Institute. I can't help with what you're looking for."

"Don't lie, Mr. Morgan. I know you're an expert on shockwaves. Fifteen years ago, the government used you for experiments in the Atlantic Ocean during underwater explosion tests on how shockwaves traveled through areas just below the surface and near the bottom of the sea. You were their star scientist. The test files became classified and were destroyed because it violated a treaty between our countries. I know all about you, Mr. Morgan. As I said a moment ago, did you hear that?"

"Hear what?"

"Your wife is screaming."

A door opened and closed from down the hall. Viktor appeared, carrying a white cloth. When he drew near enough, Boris saw the cloth had splotches of red on it.

"Give that to me."

Morgan shrunk away from the cloth, chanting the word *no* repeatedly while shaking his head back and forth.

"Mr. Morgan, please confirm this is your wife's finger," Boris said, holding the appendage in front of the scientist's face.

Morgan closed his eyes and refused to look.

"Either you confirm it's her finger, or I will remove her whole hand. Do it now."

Morgan's eyes fluttered open, tears falling from them, as he leaned forward and glimpsed the digit in the cloth. He nodded and looked away quickly, falling onto the floor and curling up. Boris heard him saying something over and over.

"What is that you're saying?" Boris asked.

Morgan glanced up at him, his eyes boring holes into him.

"I will kill you for that."

"A little anger can go a long way. Hold onto that thought, and you can certainly try if you make it out of here. Now, it's decision time. Do I continue to remove pieces from your wife's body, or will you do as you're told?"

Morgan wiped the tears from his face, got his arms under him, and lifted himself off the floor.

"I will do as you say," Morgan said, a hard tone in his voice now. "Although, I get to see my wife at least once a day until we are finished. Even kidnappers offer proof of life. Show me she's alive and well each day, and I will serve you as required."

Boris glared at the small, ridiculous American making demands after what he had just witnessed. He glanced at his men and then made a decision.

"You will do what we want, or you will never see her again." He turned to Viktor. "Make sure you present Mrs. Morgan's dead body to Mr. Morgan if he decides to stray any longer." He turned back to Morgan. "If for any reason you aren't absolutely compliant, I will kill Pat Morgan myself. Are we clear?"

Mr. Morgan nodded.

"Good. Now, before we begin." He turned his attention to his comrade. "Viktor, I need you to go and remove Bryce Jacob from our path. I understand he's checking out of the hospital tonight. He must be removed today. Run him over like you did his son. I don't care. Kill him any way you want. You Americans"—Boris slapped Mr. Morgan's back rather hard, making the scientist stumble a few steps—"too stupid for your own good. I thought killing the man's son would've been enough to get him off our ass. We even bought his boss, expensive though he was, but nothing has worked so far."

Boris met Viktor's unwavering gaze. "What are you waiting for? Do not come back here until Jacob is dead."

He started for the door. "Gentlemen," he shouted. "Everyone back to work."

Chapter 18

BRYCE JACOB STOOD BY THE WINDOW of his hospital room, answering questions as other officers from internal affairs took his statement. The investigation into Sergeant William McGregor's actions would be long and intensive. The kind of investigation that he had no time for. The people behind McGregor would try again. Why they were coming after him was a mystery. Other than the hundreds of arrests he'd made on the job, no one was powerful enough to want to kill him— a detective, whoever it was, had to be extremely wealthy or powerful to have McGregor working for them.

"Tell me again what he said when he entered the room with the flowers?"

The IA idiot repeatedly asked the same questions as if he hadn't heard Jacob the first time. Jacob understood it, but now he was losing his patience.

"Look, I've gone over everything several times. Take what I've given you and go with it. Start looking into

McGregor's contacts and whatever else you can find on him. Search his phone records. I don't care. He came in here to kill me, and if it weren't for Everton, I'd be dead right now. So, if you'll excuse me, I will check on Everton's surgery."

"We're not finished here, Mr. Jacob."

"Detective."

"What?"

"It's Detective Jacob. And yes, we are finished. I'm checking out of the hospital today. If you need me, you know where you can find me."

Jacob limped through the throng of people dusting for prints and taking photographs. At the nurses' station, he asked where he'd find Steven Wallace and Maria Lopez. The nurse said she wasn't allowed to give out that kind of information unless he was family, but since she knew him, she'd just let him read the computer screen.

Armed with their room numbers, he ran to Maria's door first. After knocking gently, he opened the door.

Maria lay on her bed, eyes closed.

He approached the bed and whispered, "Are you awake?"

"Yes." She opened her eyes. "Oh, it's you."

"Great to see you, too." Jacob smiled wide.

"When I saw you last, we were thrown about and turned into rag dolls. Tell me our meeting was coincidental."

"Absolutely."

"Absolutely what?"

"Coincidental."

"And this isn't? I mean, being in my hospital room. You have a purpose this time?"

"Yes. I wanted to ask you something strange."

"Strange?"

An awkwardness settled between them.

She eyed him suspiciously, studying his face. "What kind of strange?"

"Are you seeing things?"

"Seeing things?" she repeated, her face coloring.

That got her attention. She pulled her gaze away from him to stare out the hospital window.

"Maybe," she whispered. "What kind of things are you talking about?"

"Strange things, like visions. Feeling things, too. Like, you know what someone might be thinking. Not just thinking, though, more like you know how they feel about something?"

"No, I'm not feeling people's feelings." She fixed her attention back on him. "I am seeing things, though." She sat up higher in bed. "Do you think it has something to do with what happened to us?"

"Yes, I do. Whatever it was, they're calling it an air quake. This means that the air shook so violently that it vibrated us, vibrated our brains, which I think caused our comas. And now I'm feeling and seeing things I couldn't before. I even think that I saw my son walk by my hospital room."

"Your son? You mean he came to visit?"

"My son was killed in an accident last summer."

"I'm sorry." She stared at him a moment longer. "But you don't think it was an accident, do you?"

"See? You're feeling things. You were able to *feel* what I

meant."

Maria shrugged. "More like I perceived your meaning of the word *accident* by your tone."

Jacob found the chair and pulled it closer to her bed to take a seat. This was the most he'd used his legs since waking from the coma, and they felt slightly uncomfortable.

"Can you tell me what you've seen?"

Maria clasped her hands together on her stomach, then nodded.

"There was a woman in that bed over there." Maria pointed. "The woman woke up, said she felt great, then left the room. Minutes later, doctors came running in to revive her. She had died, and the woman I spoke to was her spirit after it left her body. I know that sounds crazy, but I think that's what happened." A tear slipped from one eye. "Not knowing it at first was spooky. I didn't believe it—still don't. But then …"

More tears came. Jacob grabbed the tissue box by the bed and offered her one. She wiped her eyes and continued.

"Then I saw a heart with an arrow drawn through it in the condensation on the window. My husband's and my initials were inside the heart. John, my husband, used to do that all the time. He's been dead for almost a year, too."

Jacob lowered his head and considered what Maria had just said. If it was true, which he was convinced it was, then what happened to them allowed Maria and himself to see someone from the other side, which meant that he had actually seen his son or at least the spirit of his son. Although, even without Maria's comments, he had already gathered that it was Lance because how many boys looking exactly like his son would be walking throughout the hospital with a Frisbee in hand?

That meant Steven Wallace was also going through some form of this event, which might prove even more worrisome as he was an unstable individual to begin with.

Jacob stood momentarily, leaned on the back of the chair, and then moved to the end of Maria's bed, where he stopped. Over his shoulder, he glanced at her.

"Has anyone come to visit you with any kind of message?"

Maria glanced down at her hands. After a moment, she looked back at Jacob and shook her head in the negative.

"I had a woman come into my room. She told me her name was Ulea. Apparently, I'm supposed to speak to someone named Kramer Kay. I understand that this Kay woman will help us through what has happened to us." He paused, wondering if he should say the rest, then decided to. "I wonder how Wallace is dealing with all this."

"The guy who attacked me?"

Jacob nodded.

"Who cares about him after what he did?"

"I understand how you feel, but Wallace is harmless. I've arrested him twice. He's a good informant on the street, but sometimes, he gets too involved and needs to be hauled in. I went to the Amy Greg Center to meet with him that day."

Maria stared out the window.

Jacob watched her a moment. "Listen, we need to talk more about this. Wait for me. I'm going to see Wallace, and I'll come back. Are you planning on leaving the hospital anytime soon?"

Maria nodded. "In a couple of hours. I want to sleep in my own bed tonight."

"Okay, if I miss you, can I call you at home?"

Maria nodded again. "Of course."

Jacob wrote down her number, gave her his cell number, then left the room.

He headed to the other floor where they were keeping Steven Wallace.

A uniformed officer sat reading a newspaper on a chair outside Wallace's room. It would be impossible to know all the cops on the force, so Jacob identified himself.

The officer nodded. "I recognize the name as one of the others involved in the accident."

"That's me. Look, I need a word with Wallace."

The officer waved at the door. "Be my guest. He's handcuffed to the bed. Nothing to worry about."

Jacob wasn't worried but thanked the officer anyway.

He cracked open the door, stepped into the gloomy room, and shut the door behind him. His vision took a moment to adjust to the room as all the lights were off, and only a soft glow came through the curtains.

He quickly determined only one person was in the room —but that person wasn't in the bed. This all came to him as if he could perceive it through telepathy. This new version of perception would come in handy at his job.

Eyes adjusted now, Jacob saw that the bed was empty.

"Steve?" he whispered.

"Yeah?" came the soft reply from the corner under the window.

Jacob moved around the bed and saw Wallace curled up

on the floor, his knees drawn to his chest, one arm wrapped around his knees, the other dangling from the bar on the side of the bed.

"You doing okay?"

"Yeah."

"How are you feeling?"

"Not good."

"Why?"

"Because."

This was how conversations with addicts sometimes went. One sentence answers.

"Do you think we could talk for a bit?" Jacob stepped all the way around the bed.

"No."

"No? Why not?"

"Just no."

"Something bothering you, Steve?"

"Nothing to talk about."

"I'm not here to discuss what happened or what charges they are bringing against you. I want to talk about how you've felt since you got here."

Steve lifted his head and looked at Jacob. The man had been crying.

"How I'm feeling? Why would you care?"

"Because something happened to us out there that day by the river, and I think it happened to all of us the same. I want to talk about it, and I want to help you with it."

"How could you help me? Why would you *want* to help me?"

"Because whatever is happening to us could drive

someone mad. I'll go first." Jacob leaned against the bed. "I'm seeing things."

Even in the dim light, he detected Wallace's look of surprise.

"I'm seeing stuff, too."

So it was true. Whatever happened had affected all three of them.

"What kind of stuff?" he asked.

"A man was here. Then he disappeared."

"You mean, like, left the room."

"No, like disappeared. Right in front of me. However, that's unimportant, and I don't want to discuss it. What he told me is what is important."

"What did he tell you?" Jacob asked as he jostled upward until he was partially sitting on the end of the bed. It would be a few more days before his legs returned to a hundred percent.

"He told me that I was going to die, and so were a lot of people unless I helped you. Since I'm not that interested in meeting Lucifer yet, I've decided to help you. Maybe it'll redeem some of the shit I've done in my life." Wallace shrugged and cast his glance downward. "The man who came with the message said I was going to die anyway." His voice took on a saddened tone. "I've decided to do something right for once. I want to die with some kind of honor."

Jacob stared down at him. "Well, I'd love to have your help. But let's focus on staying alive. That work for you?"

Wallace nodded and started to cry.

Chapter 19

"I GIVE YOU MY WORD," BORIS said. "No more harm will come to you or your wife if you comply with our wishes. This'll be over quite soon."

Morgan nodded and glanced up at Boris. "We're not going to leave here alive, are we?"

"Of course you are. I don't care if you've seen my face. This isn't like in the movies. When our task is completed, we will already be outside the United States, far away from any chance of imprisonment by your authorities. And the cool part, as you Americans say, is we have what you call a scapegoat. Someone else will be taking the blame."

Morgan stood from his chair. "I have your word?"

"Absolutely." Boris stared directly at Dan. The intensity of his gaze always fooled prisoners because they clung to hope too much. The only thing that separated man from an animal was hope. Because of that, many men had died, hoping they wouldn't. The man before him was no different.

Offer him his life, sincerely offer it to him, convince him he would be fine, and the man would do anything for him.

"Okay," Morgan said, nodding. "The physics of your bomb are incorrect. Also, who told you to place it in water?"

Morgan walked past Boris, heading into the main control room. Boris followed, impressed with Morgan's take-charge attitude.

"Tell me, what is wrong with what we have done?"

Morgan turned around to address Boris. "It's the pressure of the explosion that's dangerous to humans because of the obvious—it does what happened last week to those three people. The shockwave hit them and tossed them around like toys. It probably did temporary damage to their ears, too. So, if someone were to stand behind a large rock or tree, they could potentially be unhurt, even if they're quite close to your device at the time of detonation."

Morgan spoke with his hands a lot, Boris noticed. Both hands enunciated various words as he continued.

"Before I go into this"—he turned and raised his voice— "I want everyone working on this shockwave device to come closer." As Morgan waited for the few stragglers to enter the control room, he flipped a couple of switches and adjusted a nozzle, most of which Boris knew little about. That's what his scientists were for.

"Okay, here's a little of how it goes." Morgan pointed at the wall. "It takes about fifty pounds per square inch to push in a wall and about ten pounds per square inch to push in a window. Most of you know this already, but if you intended to hurt the Amy Greg Detox Center building, then you failed miserably because, by the time the effect of this bomb hit the wall of the detox center, it was exhausted as their windows only cracked. Some broke, sure, but not as many as needed for the effect you're looking for."

A couple of the men were nodding. Boris felt a certain level of accomplishment as he listened to one of the top American bomb technicians schooling his men. He did this. He got Dan Morgan. His superiors were going to promote him when he got home.

"I once witnessed a man twenty-five feet from a bomb out in the open but lying on the ground. He not only remained conscious after detonation, but he was able to get up immediately after the explosion to start helping the wounded. Now, as we all know, a shockwave from an underwater blast will travel faster and farther—six thousand feet per second versus one thousand feet per second in the air. Also, it's dealing with much higher pressures, which are measured in tons per square inch instead of pounds."

Morgan paused to look around and make sure everyone was following him. Boris watched. No one had a question.

"Continue," Boris said.

"The effect of a shockwave in water is greatest on deeply submerged objects and least on those on the surface because the surface can yield to the wave. So, the effect is practically nil on the surface of the water itself."

Boris cleared his throat. "Help us understand why. Our technology has been tested and proven to work. I'm not sure what you're saying."

"The center of the charge is our origin of reference. When this charge is detonated, a spherical shockwave is produced, which propagates in all directions. When an explosion happens, if the pressure wave is fast enough to break the sound barrier, it generates a powerful shockwave. But this can only be achieved in the air and not underwater."

"I was led to believe that since the effect was so much greater in the water, we could hide the bomb in a body of water and set it off remotely by cellular. We understood that such proximity to the detox building would have at least some of the desired effects. How come the wave didn't ruin their bodies on the spot?"

"Underwater, when the shockwave reaches your skin, it will pass through you. Little of its power would be reflected because your body's density is similar to water's. This doesn't happen in the air. Besides, we're getting off-topic. There is something unique to your technology that I haven't figured out. As you're most likely all aware, they're calling what happened an air quake. Your bomb did little damage other than to shake the air violently."

"There was a whole lotta shakin' going on," one of the men whispered.

"Is that some kind of American humor?" Boris asked.

"Look," Morgan cut in. "All I know is you will need a different device than the one you used out there, or you might end up with only a powerful shake again."

Boris shook his head and stepped closer to Dan. "Out of the question. It is too timely and risky to ship in the parts to build what we need. There were two devices. The smaller one was used in the detox center. The larger one will be employed on Saturday. Work with what you've got. Make this happen with what you have at your disposal, Mr. Morgan, so you and your lovely wife can go home safe."

Morgan stared at him a moment, then nodded. "Okay, I will do as you say, but I can't make promises on levels of success based on what I have to work with."

Boris glared at him. "Your work will produce the results I need, or you and your wife will be tortured and dismembered. Do I make myself clear?"

Dan Morgan nodded again, then turned away and got back to work.

Chapter 20

"WALLACE, IT'S GOING TO BE OKAY," Bryce Jacob said.

Steve looked up at him. "How's that? How will seeing phantoms and probably dying next week be okay?"

"I don't think you have to die."

"Oh, okay. Cool."

"No, seriously. I had a visitor with a message, too. She told me to find a woman named Kramer Kay. Apparently, she'll be able to help us understand what's happening. Also, if whoever they are is warning us and telling us what to do, it's because they want us to succeed. That means they think we have a chance at succeeding." Jacob stood up from the bed and walked to the window of Wallace's room, where he drew the curtains back to allow more light. "I think I saw my son earlier. Having this vision of the other side and seeing him again would be a blessing all by itself."

"Yeah, well, I don't want any more visions, I don't want to die, and I don't want any blessings."

Jacob looked over at him. "But you agree to work with me and not against me?"

Steve nodded. "Yes, I will work with you. I have no idea what we're supposed to do, but I've been an informant to you for some time now. What's one more job that could save my life or my soul?"

Jacob turned to him. "I have a couple of conditions. No drugs, no booze."

Steve nodded.

"No, I need to hear it. Do we have a deal?"

"Yes. Deal."

"Also, you do as I tell you. You have to listen to me. Think of it like you're my deputy."

"I don't want to be no fucking cop."

"You know what I mean. Is that acceptable to you?"

"Yes."

"Okay, last condition. Maria will probably join us since this thing happened to her, too. You will have to apologize for scaring the shit out of her, and after that, you will be respectful and courteous to her. Are we agreed?"

Wallace nodded. "Agreed. But what are we doing? I mean, what is it you want us working on?"

"Stand up. Don't worry about that right now. First, we have to talk about how we can break a few laws."

The frown on Wallace's face amused Jacob.

"What are you talking about now?"

"You're in custody. You won't get bail this time. There's a cop outside your door—"

"Yeah. So?"

"That means I have to break you out of custody. How

does tomorrow sound?"

"Now you're talking," Wallace said. He clapped his hands together and smiled at Jacob. "That's what I was trying to do before we got knocked over by the air quake."

"It'll work this time." Jacob smiled and glanced down at the solitary handcuff. "Trust me."

Chapter 21

DAN MORGAN WAS RUNNING OUT OF time. He didn't trust his captors at all. There was no way they were going to let him and his wife leave their underground facility alive. So, from the moment they arrived, he'd been watching and studying their routines, mentally working on a plan to escape if possible. For starters, they were in the basement of a large complex. He assumed from the comings and goings of the men here that the building above them was probably a manufacturing plant of some kind, and almost all of the people up there had no idea what was down here. He'd gathered that by the secrecy in which the employees came and went—private elevators, private stairwells that led outside somehow.

He assumed they'd be in the clear if they could make it to the elevators. The only way to do that was to grab his wife, snatch an elevator pass off one of the scientists, make it to the level above them, and blow the whistle.

Yeah, right. Only in the movies.

"What's that?" one of the men standing a few feet away asked.

Dan glanced over, not knowing he spoke out loud. "Oh, nothing. Just talking to myself." Then, an idea hit him. "How long have you been down here?"

The man looked up at him. "Shut up. No talking. Do what you have to do. If you need me, I'm here. Other than that, we don't talk."

Dan shrugged to show the guy his words didn't bother him, but it confirmed Morgan's theory—they had to get out of there immediately while Boris was busy in his office in the building above. Also, that Viktor guy was out hunting Bryce Jacob, who seemed to infuriate Boris.

There was no plan, no time to think. He was a dead man. His wife would be killed, too. They'd already mutilated her. All Dan had to do was help them build a bomb that would kill people—women and children. This was something he couldn't be a part of. With his death sentence already confirmed, Dan was left with no choice but to try to escape. If they made it, then great, but if they killed them while attempting to escape, waiting to die was over, and maybe it would delay the work on the device.

He stepped over to the end of the console and appeared to be studying some of the raw data streaming there. A final look around the area confirmed only two scientists and one guard were on duty somewhere. Probably having dinner. They had nothing to worry about with a compliant scientist, not to mention every exit needed a pass of some kind to access it.

He knelt and picked up the fire extinguisher near his feet.

One of Boris's men stood ten feet away. Dan's stomach churned, and his legs weakened, but he was a hunter. He'd killed animals in the bush, and weren't these vile men just animals?

Fueled by rage and self-preservation, not concerned whether he would kill the guy or not, Dan moved in, closing the gap. Six feet became five, then four, then three.

When the man glanced his way, Dan Morgan already had the extinguisher raised and ready.

When he thrust it forward, it connected just below the man's left cheekbone. Dan pushed the extinguisher so hard into the other guy's face that he lost his grip, and it bounced off the console, spun in the air, and clattered to the floor.

The extent of the damage to the man was brutal. He had dropped to the floor and was convulsing, his limbs shaking. The man's jaw sat askew, dislocated at the bottom of his mouth, his cheek dented in where the bone had broken. He moaned and looked up at Dan with one good eye, the other eye sunken behind where the broken cheekbone had moved in front of it. Blood now seeped from the split skin that wrapped the broken bones.

With no time to dawdle, Dan grabbed at the man's elevator pass, unclipping it from the guy's lab coat. He bent over the man whose moaning had increased in volume and grabbed the extinguisher. After unclipping the hose, he was ready to pump the foam if anyone tried to stop him.

He ran for the prison area where Patricia was being held. There, he found the other scientist. At first, Dan wasn't sure if Boris's scientists worked with him or were kidnapped, but he soon learned they all worked for Boris.

The man didn't seem to want to fight. He just stared at Dan without moving. He didn't say a word or attempt to stop Dan.

After trying both doors and finding them locked, he shouted Pat's name but got no response.

Precious time slid by. He still didn't know where the armed guard was. Each minute was closer to his death.

He spun around and saw the scientist was on the phone now.

"Put it down!" Dan shouted.

The scientist lowered the phone.

"Where are they holding my wife?"

The man pointed upstairs. "In a room on the fourth floor beside Boris's office."

"Shit."

Dan spun on his heels and ran for the elevator. He pushed the button and waited. A quick look back and the weird scientist was still staring at him, his phone back at his ear. His lips were moving as he spoke to someone.

The elevator doors opened.

The guard stepped off, chewing a sandwich, a newspaper in his hand.

Without hesitation, Dan raised the end of the hose and depressed the handle. At that precise second, the guard dropped his sandwich and newspaper, but white foam raced out of the hose and into the guard's mouth and eyes before the guy even had a chance to cover his face.

Dan covered the guard in foam, then kicked him aside as the elevator doors started to close. He slipped between them, then jabbed at the number four and mashed the CLOSE DOOR button.

The doors closed, but the elevator didn't move. He couldn't catch a breath. He had hit the number four. Why wasn't he ascending?

The doors opened into the chamber again. The guard was getting up off the floor, coughing and hacking. Dan watched as the guard reached into his jacket and withdrew a gun.

The doors closed again, and he hit four harder this time.

Nothing happened.

The pass card!

"Shit!" he grunted, then swiped the card, and the number four button stayed alight.

The elevator moved and began ascending, but not before a loud bang and a hollow echo.

The guard had fired his weapon into the elevator doors, but Dan was already past that level.

Seconds later, the doors opened on floor number four. He stood there in utter shock at the normalcy he witnessed before him. An office with cubicles and people on phones with headsets, others chatting away to each other, oblivious to what was happening below them.

Locked in the grip of unreality. Insane with the fear, wild-eyed, and covered in sweat, Dan stepped from the elevator.

He approached the woman at a desk closest to him.

"Are you all mad?"

She examined him, the extinguisher in his hands, then met his gaze.

"Is everything okay, Mister? Is there a fire?"

To see a normal office setting in a building where they were building bombs was so off-putting that he couldn't think for a moment.

"I'm looking for a man named Boris. Where can I find him?"

A confused look crossed her face. "Boris? There's no Boris here. You must have the wrong floor or the wrong building."

"No, I'm in the right place. This is his company. He has my wife, and I was building a bomb for him."

The woman backed away, her chair wheeling from her desk. Other people were watching now. Good, this was what he wanted—to make a scene.

The point of no return had been reached in the basement when he broke the scientist's face. There was no going back.

"I assure you, I'm telling you the truth."

"Let me get someone who can help you."

She jumped from her chair and disappeared behind a partition. She placed a phone to her ear, glanced his way, and then spoke into it. He could swear he read the word *security* on her lips.

He kicked the corner of her desk, knocking dividers to the floor.

She jumped and dropped the phone.

"I'm not fucking joking here. Where's Boris? I can't believe you people." He glanced around in a circle. "Everyone listen. Your bosses are murderers. Do you hear me?" He was shouting now.

"I hear you," a man said. "And I'd like to help."

Dan turned to the speaker.

It was Boris.

"There you are, you piece of shit."

"Now, take it easy. Is this a customer complaint? Were you recently employed with us?"

Standing less than four feet away, Boris acted as if nothing was amiss.

"Are you kidding? Where's my wife? I know you're holding her on this floor. Where is she?"

The woman moved forward. "Hector, I'm sorry. He came off the elevator and—"

"It's okay, Janice. I'm sure I'll be able to help this man, or I'll have security deal with it."

"Don't you dare talk about me like I'm delusional. You kidnapped my wife and me. Where the fuck is she?" Dan raised the hose of the extinguisher.

Boris/Hector stepped back, hands out in front of him. "Whoa, take it easy. There's no need to get upset. I'm sure we can figure this out."

Dan pushed the lever and sprayed foam at Boris. It hit him around the chest area. Movement caught his eye, and he turned, but it was too late.

Armed security had arrived. Two burly men smashed into Dan, sending the extinguisher from his hands, the flow of white foam ceasing as his grip released the handle. He hit the floor with one guard on top of him and the other trying to grab his arms.

Dan was consumed with rage at that moment as he struggled. He screamed, rolled, punched, and gouged with everything he had in him. He got a lucky jab at the guard's face, then the guy rolled to the side, his right eye bleeding, his scream a piercing cry.

The other security officer was unclipping something from his belt loop.

Dan spun on his hip on the carpeted floor and kicked at the man's ankles. The guard's legs collapsed as he dropped to his knees, then he sprawled out on the floor.

Dan pushed up off the floor and jumped up to his feet. The few people who had converged to watch the skirmish stepped back, unsure what Dan would do now. Boris wiped at his face, moaning while rubbing his eyes. A woman had offered him a towel, which he used in a cubicle about ten feet away.

Dan raised his foot and dropped it on the guard's face. Then again, then once more until the guard stopped moving.

He grabbed the gun at the guard's waist and spun to the other man whose eye was covered in blood now.

"Where is she?" Dan shouted, the weapon held high.

A woman screamed, and most of the audience scattered at the sight of the gun.

"You are mistaken," Boris said. "Whomever it is you're looking for isn't here." He set the napkins down and stared red-faced at Dan, his eyes blinking in irritation. "More security will be here momentarily. You cannot possibly expect to fight everyone. You will not leave this building alive."

"I don't have to fight everyone. Just you."

Dan aimed at Boris and pulled the trigger.

Nothing happened.

He glanced at the gun and pulled the trigger again, but still nothing happened.

Movement to his left caught his eye, but he was too late. Someone smashed into him, a monster grip wrapping around his neck. He couldn't breathe, his vision blurred. Gagging for air, his consciousness wavered. Then he was being dragged, his heels sliding over the carpet.

The forearm relaxed, and he gasped in the air as the elevator doors closed. Were they headed back to the basement?

The man holding him allowed his feet to touch the ground, and he breathed in deeper.

Moments later, the doors opened again, and he was dragged out of the elevator. They were in the lobby of a regular office building.

Two guards ran up to them. One of them was talking into a radio in his hand.

"We'll take him from here," one of the new guards said.

The man holding him spoke so close to Dan's ear that he winced at the volume.

"Where are you going to hold him until the police arrive? Will you need more help?"

"No, that's fine. We won't be involving the police."

"But he assaulted our people upstairs, and he used a fire extinguisher on Hector. If the weapon were working, he would've shot Hector."

The man released Dan, and the other two men grabbed his arms and held him tight.

"This is no longer your concern. Hector has ordered us to remove this man from the building. Take any other questions you have up with Hector."

Dan was yanked and pulled toward the double glass

doors that led to the outside.

This was too easy. They wouldn't just let him go. Even if they had killed Patricia, how would they finish their device without him?

The doors opened automatically, and Dan was shoved outside. He stumbled on wobbly legs and fell to the pavement, scuffing an elbow, the sharp sting making him wince.

When he looked back up, the doors were closing. The guard locked them and stared through the glass at Dan. He then took his finger and ran it across the neckline of his shirt, indicating the throat area and where to cut. The international symbol of *you're dead*.

Dan rolled to his side and got to his feet. Escaping Boris without Patricia all but guaranteed she would be killed. Dan wept as he walked, trying to get as far away from the building as possible.

He had no doubt Boris wasn't finished with him yet, but they had to make a public display of removing him from the building.

Boris didn't know that Dan Morgan wasn't done with him either.

As long as Morgan could cross the river and get inside the detox center, he could call the authorities and tell them everything he knew.

They would have to send a team of armed men into Boris's basement and end the madness.

And stop anyone from hurting Patricia.

He just hoped he wouldn't be too late.

Chapter 22

DETECTIVE BRYCE JACOB LEFT STEVEN WALLACE with a story. Wallace needed to complain of chest pains and headaches to remain in the hospital for at least one more night. Jacob would return and remove him from police custody, although he hadn't figured out how to do that yet.

In the meantime, Jacob would talk to Maria Lopez and try to locate this Kramer Kay woman he was supposed to talk to.

Jacob reached Maria's room again and entered after knocking softly.

The room was empty.

"Shit!"

He ran over to the nurses' counter.

"Excuse me, can you tell me when Maria left?"

The nurse looked up. "Are you a family member?"

"I'm Detective Jacob. I was brought in with her. Now tell me, when did she fucking leave?"

"I'm sorry, sir. She asked for privacy." The woman spoke with an indignant tone.

"For fucks sake! Just tell me—"

"Must I call hospital security?" The woman placed a hand on the phone.

"Fuck," he muttered, then turned away to head back to his room. It was late in the evening, but a few people were collecting whatever they could from the murder scene in his room.

Someone had placed his clothes on the bed. He walked over to them and started to get dressed, his limp less pronounced.

Could the three people affected by that air quake now be targets? Would someone come after them to finish the job? If so, he couldn't tell Steve that theory. He couldn't handle it, and he was in police custody, so he was the safest of the three of them. But Maria needed to be brought up to date on what Jacob knew, and if she was in danger, she also needed to be made aware of that.

Without worrying whether anyone was watching, he dropped the hospital gown, pulled his pants up, and slipped on the collared shirt he had worn that fateful day almost two weeks ago.

"Wait, where are you going?"

Richard Cranston, the man who always wanted Sergeant McGregor's job, stepped into the room.

"Home. Anywhere but here."

"Have they got your statement?"

"Of course they do."

Cranston eyed him. "I'm taking over until things can be

ironed out. You gonna have a problem with that?"

Jacob shook his head. "Nope."

"Good. Stick around town. I'll want to talk to you soon. This will bruise the department's profile and won't go away easily."

"Not my issue."

"Just stick around town."

"I'm not going anywhere." Jacob headed for the door.

"Hey, Jacob, hold up."

He stopped at the door and turned back to look at Cranston.

"Look, this may be a difficult question, but someone has to ask it."

Jacob nodded for Cranston to go ahead.

"I've been hearing that McGregor was pretty hard on you. Apparently, he wanted to suspend you. Wasn't there a warning in there recently, too?"

"Something like that. So, what are you saying? You want to suspend me, too?"

Cranston held up his hands. "Hey, I'm just looking for someone McGregor pissed off, and I'm hearing around town that you were the one he was gunning for—"

"Fuck you, Cranston."

Jacob stepped out of the room and started down the hall. He shouted over his shoulder. "Great detective work, Rich. Rumors will always lead you to the murderer. Just keep listening to what they're saying, whatever the fuck it is, and you'll solve everything." Then under his breath, he whispered, "Asshole."

Chapter 23

THE HOUSE SEEMED EMPTIER SOMEHOW, DARKER, as Maria parked out front. She exited her car, shuffled up the short steps, and opened the front door with her keys. After shutting and locking the door firmly, she turned on the hall lights and glanced over at the altar.

It sat as she'd left it—decrepit looking, candle wax gelled in its act of dripping over the wooden ledge, candles almost stubs now.

"Shit, I forgot to buy new candles." She set her purse down. "So, it's been almost two weeks, and a lot has happened in that time."

There was no response. She was alone without ghosts to haunt her.

Exhausted, weak, and sore, Maria began to undress in the living room, tossing her shirt and pants on the sofa, then headed for the kitchen, where she poured a glass of her favorite red wine.

With a glass in hand, eyes half-lidded, she entered the bathroom and drew a hot bath. When it was almost full, she removed her bra and panties, then eased into the water and sipped her wine again before resting her head back. She placed her feet under the water, still rushing from the tap to soothe them.

Maria turned off the tap with her toes as the water neared the tub's edge.

The final drips from the tap ceased, and the house was silent.

Like clothing moving against itself, a soft ruffle sounded from the hallway outside the bathroom.

Maria opened her eyes and sat up, water sloshing around her. She waited a heartbeat for the water to settle, listening to the house.

"Hello?"

There was no response. Should she have checked the house when she got home? She had been gone for two weeks, and anything could've happened, but would someone break in and *live* there in that time? Highly unlikely.

The noise came again. This time, it sounded like someone said something under their breath.

Goosebumps rose on her arms, and the hair on her neck lifted. Should she get out and investigate? Or was she imagining things?

"Is anyone there?" she shouted, her own voice startling her.

This had to be the worst place in the house for her. Sitting stark naked in the bathtub, vulnerable to any intruder, exhausted and drinking. She was more ready for bed than a fight.

Something clunked from somewhere in the house. It sounded like a soft thud on the carpet just outside the bathroom door.

Maria covered her mouth to quell the short scream she almost released.

That was enough to get her moving.

Someone was definitely in her house—someone or something. For all she knew, rats could have gnawed their way inside while she was away.

Sitting naked in the tub wasn't going to solve anything.

She got up quickly and wrapped a towel around herself while dabbing her skin as she stepped from the water. She stepped to the bathroom door with the towel covering her body and slowly peeked around the corner.

The hallway was empty.

On the balls of her feet, Maria made it to her bedroom, where she opened her dresser and retrieved clean underwear. Her stomach clenched and her hands were shaking. She had no idea what made the noise or if someone was in her house.

When she'd gotten home, she was exhausted after all the trauma and weeks of recovery. But now she was wide awake and on full alert.

The drawer with her bras was the loud one. She eased it open with only the smallest protest. It took her minutes to get fully dressed.

After a quick scan of the bedroom in search of a weapon, she spied the umbrella. It would have to do. Umbrella in hand, she moved to the door and glanced out into the hallway again. Then she waited for a minute, then another, watching for someone or something to show themselves. It was almost eleven p.m., and her weariness was taking hold, her patience wavering.

Self-doubting took over. What if she didn't hear anything? There'd been no sound since she left the bathtub. Perhaps she was imagining it, and the clunking sound was all in her head.

The alarm clock by her bed clicked on at full volume, making her scream and jump. She spun around so fast that the umbrella hit the wall. She bumped her head, then dropped to her butt on the carpeted floor. The alarm was driving her nuts. She scrambled to her feet and ran to it, smacking the top to turn it off.

"Why the fuck," she gasped, "was that thing set to go off at eleven at night?" She released a frustrated scream at the empty room.

Then, it all came rushing back to her. Two weeks ago, when she was home last, she had been sleeping more during the day and getting up at eleven at night to spend long hours watching TV, reading, and taking walks alone. Eleven was the time her dead husband, John, used to come home from work. They would stay up until three or four in the morning sipping wine together, watching movies, and making love. She missed him so much that she was keeping to their old schedule.

The alarm clock's display read 11:01 p.m.

A wave of grief swept over her. If only John were with her.

She heard the distinctive sound of a match being struck somewhere behind her. Her stomach clutched as she glanced at her hands, and they were empty. The umbrella was by the bedroom door, and someone was still in the house.

Maria ran over, grabbed the umbrella, and peeked around the corner into the hallway. It was empty, so she stepped out of the bedroom, the umbrella raised above her head, gripped in both hands like a sword.

Why didn't she call 911 right away? What was she waiting for?

She needed visual confirmation. Why call the cops if she was just hearing things?

There was the woman from the hospital room that she had to consider as well—that dead woman walking. What if this was another case like that? And if it was, what could the cops do then? Actually, what the hell would she do?

Maria made it down the hall unimpeded. Light flickered near the living room alcove. She stopped short to take a breather.

The candles were all burned out when she got home. There had been no flame. And yet now, the flickering light against the walls ahead made it seem that someone had lit the candles. If that were true, why would someone do that?

Instead of moving into the living room, she stepped back a couple of feet and entered the den. After a quick look around, she saw it was empty. The phone sat on John's desk. She snatched it up and moved back into the hallway. With a finger hovering over the buttons, ready to call the police, she edged around the door frame and peered into the living room.

The altar to her dead husband was lit.

Both candles were burning now.

She wanted to scream. She wanted to rampage

throughout the house, shouting and swinging the umbrella. But to what end?

Controlling the urge to run around like a madwoman, she remained silent at the wall and stared into every corner of the living room but saw no one lurking about, yet someone had to be there. And it had to be someone from this side, not the other side. There was no way a ghost could light a candle, or could they?

Her pants from earlier were on the couch. That cop's phone number was in the right front pocket. She took one more look around, certain no one was about to grab her, then ran for the couch, where she snatched up her pants. In a frenzied madness, her hands almost dropping the pants twice, she yanked out the number and dialed.

He answered on the second ring.

"It's Maria Lopez from the hospital."

"Are you okay? You sound upset or out of breath."

Maria glanced over her shoulder, placing her back on the wall by the couch. "I think someone's in my house," she whispered.

"Have you called the police?"

Through the phone, she detected the man was in a car. The engine's noise abated as he slowed down.

"No, I didn't want to be embarrassed if I was wrong."

The engine noise died off. The cop had stopped driving.

"What makes you think someone is there?"

"I heard noises. Clothes rustling. Something dropped somewhere, and when I went to investigate, someone lit the two candles I have set up in my living room."

"Tell me, where do you live? I need an address."

She told him.

"I'm twenty minutes away. Would you like me to come and have a look around?"

"Yes, please."

"I'm on my way, but on one condition."

She heard the engine revving again.

"What's that?"

"You call the police if anything else happens. There's a good chance they could get there faster than I could. Deal?"

"Okay. But hurry. I'm scared."

"On my way. Oh, and Maria."

"Yeah?" Her voice cracked.

"Wait outside for me."

The engine revved again, and then the line died.

Maria set the phone down beside her, already feeling better.

Something moved near the kitchen.

She looked over at the alcove that led back into the hallway.

Someone was standing there. The silhouette of a man stood in the shadows.

Maria moved backward to the front door.

The man edged forward until only his shoulder was visible in the candlelight.

Maria grabbed the knob, twisted it, and screamed as she opened the door and ran outside.

Two houses away, she looked over her shoulder and slowed to a jog. No one was chasing her.

She moved onto the front lawn of her neighbor's house to wait for the cop and catch her breath. After a full minute, she stared back at her house, whispering to herself repeatedly how everything would be okay.

"Everything would be okay." She wiped her forehead. "It had to be."

A premonition, something akin to a déjà vu, came over her.

It said things were going to get worse soon.

Real soon.

Chapter 24

Someone was following him. Jacob was sure of it now. As soon as he left the hospital, he detected a tail—actually *felt* it more than saw the tail.

After watching his mirrors for five minutes, he identified the vehicle following him.

When he pulled over to talk with Maria, a small black minivan had also pulled over a hundred meters back. Near the end of their phone call, Jacob performed a U-turn to head toward Maria's address, and the black minivan did a U-turn right after he drove by them.

They were obviously following him, unconcerned if he knew about it. That thought worried him. Could Sergeant Cranston have sent a couple of boys to keep an eye on him, or was it the people Sergeant McGregor worked for? Either way, their brazen techniques, without a care in the world that they were following a detective concerned him.

After driving two blocks, he took a hard right and a quick

left before the minivan reached the corner.

His cell phone rang again.

Could Maria be calling him back?

On the next corner, his tires squealed in protest.

Then he grabbed his cell and checked the display—private caller.

When Maria called, her name appeared on the screen, so why would she block her number? He didn't have time to take calls from blocked numbers at almost midnight. He had to focus on losing the tail before getting to Maria's house. Leading them—whoever *they* were—to her would be a mistake.

He tossed his phone onto the passenger seat. He managed two more turns before checking his mirrors and not seeing the minivan.

He unclipped the seatbelt, then leaned over and felt under the front of the passenger seat. His spare gun was right where it was supposed to be.

When he sat back up, the van was in his mirror again.

"Shit!"

He hit the gas and accelerated away. The van sped up, keeping their distance but not afraid to show their presence.

It was time to confront them, but he wanted a busier road away from residential. Once he found a crowded area with cars coming and going, he would pull over and approach them, armed.

His cell phone rang again. The minivan was so close that if Jacob slammed on the brakes, they'd hit him.

"Why the hell are you guys so close?" he shouted.

The cell phone ringtone was driving him insane. It was a

private caller again. Connected with Bluetooth, he tapped the button on the steering wheel to answer the call and end the annoying ringtone.

"What?" he barked.

His head slammed back, and his hands came off the wheel momentarily as his car jolted forward. Jacob readjusted himself and clung to the wheel, righting the vehicle.

The bastards had rammed him from behind.

"What the fuck!"

He watched his mirror. The minivan was revving its engine and heading toward his bumper again.

The vehicles made contact again. His gun kicked out from under the seat beside him. It now lay beside his cell phone in the footwell of the passenger side. One quick look over his shoulder, and he determined he had enough time to grab his weapon before they rammed him again. He lunged over and downward, stretching his arm to snatch up the gun and the phone with one swipe.

When he righted himself, the van was about ten feet behind him. Jacob set the gun between his legs, focused on his steering, and turned up the volume of his speakers.

"Who is this? You still there?"

"I'm Kramer Kay."

That was the name of the woman he was supposed to meet and listen to, and now she was calling him.

"We are supposed to talk."

"Soon, but first, you should know there's a vehicle behind you. The people in that vehicle are not friendly."

"No shit." Jacob took a right turn. "Wait, how do you

know that? Are you close by?"

"I'm being told they're following you to kill you. Listen, Mr. Detective, we have to talk. You can't die yet. You have something important to do first."

"Gee, thanks, I can't die yet, eh? Well, isn't that just fucking great. Any idea when I can die? I mean, since we're discussing it and all—"

The back window of his car shattered as something punctured it.

They were shooting at him now.

Jacob almost lost control of the vehicle. He corrected his steering and saw the light change to red ahead.

"Hang on, Kramer. This is going to get a little bumpy."

He jammed on the brakes, bringing his vehicle to a full stop. The gun was still between his legs. He picked it up, flipped off the safety, and grabbed the door handle but remained seated. He angled the mirror and saw the minivan had also stopped and was sitting about fifteen feet behind him, all its doors open.

No one was in sight.

One street light illuminated the area where Jacob sat. In the shadows, he detected no movement. It was close to midnight, and the streets were quiet.

Where were the occupants of the minivan? How did they exit so fast?

He angled in such a way that he was peering over the lip of the front seat. He looked left and right but saw nothing.

Yet he was quite aware they were out there, watching, waiting—he could feel it.

His left hand was still on the door handle. He pulled it

slowly, cracking the door open a notch.

Nothing happened.

He eased it open farther. Still nothing.

Perspiration rolled down his forehead. He blinked it away as it dropped into his eye.

He inhaled deeply, glanced around the car, opened the door, and stepped onto the concrete.

Gunfire shattered the quiet evening, bullets ripping into the inside of the open door. He jumped back and lay sprawled across the front seat, gun still in his hand, checking to see if he got hit.

The cacophony ceased but left behind a ringing in his ears. The door was destroyed and ruined beyond repair. He slipped the gun in his waistband and raised his arms over his head to shove open the passenger door. He'd have to crawl out the passenger side if they were on the driver's side.

As soon as that door opened, gunfire tore into it as well, shredding the inside panel.

Jacob covered his ears and shouted as they fired endlessly into his car. Metallic clangs as bullets punched into the body of the car and high-pitched shattering as the glass broke all around him. He prayed that an unlucky ricochet wouldn't hit him in the throat or the eye and kill him by accident.

The sound of his tires blowing out and the car's movement dropping slightly on one side as they blew brought him back to the here and now. He had to get out of the death car. He also realized what a mistake it was to stop.

Whoever these people were, they were determined to kill him.

But he had to wait for the bullets to stop. Or were they approaching him, keeping him under fire so he didn't move?

Then, it all stopped as suddenly as it had started.

But he was now trapped. Both doors were wide open, yet neither was a viable exit. The shooters were no doubt reloading and were probably advancing on his position as he lay there, waiting to die.

The windshield had taken many hits but was miraculously still in place.

Hoping he wouldn't hyperventilate as his body went into a state of panic, Jacob spun around on the front seat to angle his body and get his feet up on the windshield. It took two solid kicks to break it out of its position.

Outside the car, someone was walking closer. Footsteps approached.

He was a dead man. This was his last chance.

Jacob spun on the seat and crouched low, his feet under him. He grabbed his cell phone, and without a pause to catch a breath, Jacob jumped headfirst through the broken windshield onto the hood of his car. He rolled once, then fell to the pavement in front of the vehicle, his right hand already going for the gun in his waistband.

He caught a glimpse of a man a few feet from the back door, driver's side. Jacob spun on his stomach, swung his gun around, and fired twice around the edge of the headlight.

One bullet entered the shooter's face near his nose, stunning the man to a stop. He released his weapon to swing on his shoulder strap as he staggered back into the road, clawing at his face. After a few steps backward, the man fell, moaning to himself.

Jacob dropped to look under his car. Someone was standing near the trunk of his car.

"Come on out," a man said. "We need to talk, Detective Jacob."

Jacob got his knees under him and then looked at where the shoes were. He leaned up over the hood and fired through the hole in the windshield, aiming in the direction of the assailant.

When there was no return gunfire, he glanced under the car again.

The man was sprawled out on his back by the trunk.

Jacob checked the other side of the road and saw no one around. Then he edged around the car and started for the rear, the only sound a distant siren. Someone would've heard the gunfire and called the police.

At the back of the car, he found the gunman on the ground, blood oozing from his open mouth. Jacob jumped down and grabbed the guy's lapel.

"Who sent you?" he asked.

The man gasped his last breath, then died. Jacob searched both bodies but found no identification of any kind. A search of the minivan came up empty, too.

When his phone rang, it said private again. He answered right away.

"Yeah?"

"I was worried …"

"Yeah, me too. That was close. Hey, if you knew about those guys, why didn't you warn me earlier?"

Jacob started walking. He didn't want to be there when the police showed up. They would only hold him down when he needed to get to Maria. Someone was after her, too. He guessed she was already dead, but he had to try to get there.

"I knew nothing until I called the first time. Although I've known about you for weeks. A ten-year-old boy with a Frisbee came to tell me about you. He's such a strong entity."

Jacob stopped walking. "What did you say about a boy and a Frisbee?"

"It's Lance. Your son visited me during readings to ask for my help. We must meet. Preferably, before you're killed. Where are you now?"

He started walking again. How much more could he take? What the hell was going on?

"You calling me like this—"

"Look, Bryce, we have to talk. Where are you? I assume your vehicle isn't working well anymore. I can hear you walking. Where are you?"

He told her where he was, and they chose a donut shop close by where she could pick him up.

"I was on my way to a woman's house," Jacob said. "She's in trouble and called for my help."

"I'm aware of that. I will come and get you, and we'll talk to Maria together. She needs to hear this as well."

"Okay, well fuck." He ran a hand through his hair. "Hurry then."

"Just don't die on me until I get there. Thousands of people are counting on you staying alive for the next few days."

After she hung up and he started to walk toward the donut shop, he wondered about that one sentence she had said moments ago.

He had to have heard it wrong.
She said, "preferably before you're killed."
Killed? What the fuck?

Chapter 25

Boris stood in the main computer room over the dead body of his scientist.

"How the hell did this happen?" he asked. "Dan Morgan was a scientist, not a fighter. I want to know who let him out of here."

When Boris saw Morgan on the fourth floor of the building, there was no doubt things were falling apart. His mission had worked so well and went smoothly since he'd taken it on, and now, with less than a week to completion, everything was slipping away. The job could still be done—would be done—but not as well as he wanted.

"I will tell you what to do," Ivanov said, his voice tinny over the speakerphone. "But first, tell me what you've done with the man Morgan attacked before escaping?"

"I have executed the man he hit and the security guard in the basement complex. They knew the risks."

"Do you have everything in place to complete the

mission?"

Boris dropped into his chair. "We are not ready. There was a problem with the test firing two weeks ago. That's why Morgan was here. But we will proceed anyway."

"What was the problem?"

"It didn't work in the river as previous projections speculated it would. It sent out some kind of vibration instead of the shockwave we anticipated. It was meant to kill Detective Jacob, but it didn't."

"Didn't his boss do that for us?"

"He's dead now. Jacob's alive."

"Where is Jacob now?"

"I don't know, but I have Viktor and another man out there tracking him. Jacob will be dead before the sun rises."

"Okay, listen, you have to move your schedule up. Boris, we have come a long way. There can be no more trouble. If the problem with the test bomb was that it was in the water, then set it on land somewhere in downtown Los Angeles. Find a skyscraper or a heavily populated area, but make sure we have maximum damage. Are the Cubans in place?"

"No, they're not, and they won't be until Friday. That's why we were waiting until Saturday to do this."

"That doesn't work. Blow this thing as soon as we get off the phone. Announce that all the employees upstairs are free to go home until after the weekend, as some have been traumatized because of what happened when that crazy man broke in. Then set up everything as planned to lead the authorities to Castro's brother."

"Without the Cubans in place, will the Americans believe Castro's brother sanctioned the bomb?"

"Of course. The trail you created is solid and goes all the way back to the Cuban Missile Crisis. It's the perfect plan from the beginning. We get to kill a bunch of Americans, and their anger remains directed elsewhere."

"There's one last problem I need to work out."

"What's that?"

"Remote detonation."

"I was under the assumption that they were rigged with a cellular phone activation."

"Yes, but the cell phone receiver on the largest device wasn't holding a charge. The scientists were working on it—wait, I think I've got it. I'll set it to run off the battery of the vehicle the bomb is carried in. When I call the timer with the cell, I'll have the van hooked up to turn on, like using a remote starter. There should be no problem then as a running vehicle will offer plenty of juice."

"Good. So then we're set."

"Yes, Ivanov, I imagine so. I will get tickets out of LAX for the morning and set up the vehicles tonight. Then call the device so it'll go off during the morning rush hour."

"Then we will see you tomorrow night when you arrive in Moscow, and we can toast to a successful mission completed."

Boris hung up and prepared for the end.

It was almost over.

Chapter 26

JACOB DIDN'T HAVE TO WAIT LONG. A woman with distinctive black hair flowing past her shoulders entered the donut shop and looked right at him. She called his name and motioned for him to follow her. When he got outside, she was already in her car, the passenger door open.

"Get in."

When he eased in beside her, she hit the gas, the door shutting for him.

"What's the big hurry?" Jacob asked.

"I don't know, but I'm hearing that we have run out of time."

"Run out of time? What's going on? It seems to me like a lot is happening that I don't know about."

"There is. Me too."

Jacob watched her, waiting for her to start talking.

"Are you going to tell me?"

"No. Not until we get to Maria. Easier if we do it only

once."

Jacob sat back and closed his eyes. He'd been shaky in the donut shop as the adrenaline wore off. Also, he thought he'd been seeing things. At two different times, while waiting for Kramer to show, people entered the donut shop, looked around, didn't buy anything, and then left. The issue was each time that happened, they didn't use the door—they floated through it. How was someone supposed to get used to that?

It took fifteen minutes to get to Maria's street. Kramer slowed the car and drove up the darkened block, looking left and right.

"She's out here somewhere …"

Then he saw her. She ran out from behind a tree and up to Jacob's side.

"You were much longer than I expected."

"Sorry, someone shot a hole in my schedule."

Kramer smacked his arm. "Hi, I'm his friend."

Maria nodded at her. "Well, thanks for coming. I'm so embarrassed. I should've just called the police."

"It's okay, it's okay, we're here now."

"I hate to break this up," Kramer said. "But we all need to talk."

Maria leaned down and stared across at Kramer. "There's someone in my house. Well, they're probably gone now, though."

Kramer stared up at Maria. "Maria, I'm hearing that the person in your house was just like the woman you met at the hospital."

"What?" Maria said. "I don't understand."

"Let me park, and we'll go inside."

Kramer eased the car forward and turned into Maria's driveway. They got out and waited for Maria to catch up to them.

Maria faced Jacob. "Shouldn't you go in first?"

He nodded at Kramer. "I'm starting to believe what she says," he whispered. "That whoever was in your house was trying to tell you something."

Maria frowned.

They entered the house, Kramer first, Jacob second, and moved through the living room. Jacob stared at the altar and the two lit candles as he passed it and headed for the kitchen.

Kramer moved over to the altar, set her hands on the shelf, and bowed her head. Jacob watched from where he stood by the kitchen door. Maria stayed close to the front door.

"The man here earlier did his best not to startle you." Kramer glanced up at Maria.

"He didn't do a very good job of that," Maria said.

"Come." Kramer waved at them. "Sit with me. This house has no intruders. We're safe here."

Once they were both seated, she started.

"When the accident by the river happened, the three of you had your frontal lobe vibrated to a state where, when you woke up, you could see, feel, and hear the plane we call the other side. Entities vibrate at a different rate than we do. Only a few humans are born with this gift. Some go insane, and some learn to live with it as I have."

"I don't understand most of what you just said," Maria muttered. "I mean, I saw someone in my house. A man stood right over there." She pointed at the hallway.

"I know. Come on. Put on some coffee, and let's meet the man in your house."

After coffee was served, they moved back to the living room.

"For him to see you," Kramer started, "he needed to be in the same room you were in, and because you're now able to see the other side, you'd see him, too, so he tried to go about it slowly. He's telling me he only regrets not showing his face earlier."

"Well, he can just leave my house right now. I don't want to see his face."

Kramer stared at Maria. Jacob looked back and forth between the two women.

"It's a man named John Tarkington. He's been coming here every night since he died to sit and watch you sleep."

Maria gasped and raised a hand to her mouth. She leaned forward and rested a hand on the couch.

"What did you just say? I don't under—"

"John's leaving now, but he'll return for you."

Jacob jumped in to give Maria a chance to collect herself. "What about Lance? Is he here?"

Kramer turned to him. "He's been by my side continuously for the past couple of weeks, only leaving once to visit you in the hospital. Otherwise, he won't leave me alone like a mosquito in the dark."

Jacob smiled, his eyes watering. "He's here now?"

"Yes, but like John, he won't disturb us until we're done."

"Done with what?" Jacob asked, wiping his eyes.

Maria nodded at her, a tissue in her hand. "What do we have to do?"

Kramer cleared her throat. "Within twenty-four hours, thousands of people will die in Los Angeles, and I need your help to try to stop it. A bomb will detonate somewhere downtown. I hear from my guide that the bomb *will* detonate and that we can't stop it. But there's something she's not telling me, so we have to try."

Chapter 27

Boris finished with all the preparations. The small device had been placed in the back of a company van. The last two men who knew about the project had been summoned to the underground facility and summarily shot. Boris had learned an hour ago that two unidentified men were shot and killed in a gangland-like shooting. They were found dead in the street. The authoritics had identified the car they had shot up. Detective Bryce Jacob owned it. He was nowhere to be seen as of the airing of the news.

That meant the last two people alive who knew anything about this operation were himself and Dan Morgan, who would tell the police everything he knew, leaving Boris without much time.

He scattered the incriminating documents around his office and got to the van without being stopped. Deals, transactions, and bills of lading that led to ships in the harbor supposedly used by the Cuban leader Castro now lay throughout the underground compound, making it impossible for anyone to connect this bombing to the Russians. Only Morgan knew him as Boris. Everyone else upstairs would remember him as Hector, a Cuban who made good in the United States.

He drove out of the compound with the remaining device in the back of the van en route to its final destination. Forty-five minutes later, he pulled into a parking spot at 101 Hope Street, downtown Los Angeles. Boris stared at the large sign in front of the building to his right. It read, Department of Water and Power.

He cut the engine and sat back. This was it. He could finally leave the States. Everything he had worked for was coming to an end. This bomb was bigger than the first one, and he felt confident that Los Angeles was going to have a major water problem in the morning in addition to the hundreds if not thousands, of people who would be at work in this area in the morning when the device leveled a large portion of this block.

He set to work, making sure everything was connected accurately. He tested the battery power of the cell phone that he would use to call the bomb to action and made sure that when the bomb was called, the timer was set for three minutes. Even connecting it to the van's battery was an easy task.

It was four in the morning when he finished everything he had set out to do.

He placed a sign in the window that said ON DELIVERY and exited the van, ensuring it was locked up tight.

Boris walked away from his destiny and headed for the

downtown core. His flight didn't board until eleven in the morning, giving him seven hours to kill. He decided to walk for at least two of them and then catch a cab to LAX. Doing this would make it impossible to locate the van in time if anyone could discover him and trace it back to when the taxi picked him up.

There was no way anyone could stop him now. Even if Dan Morgan spilled his guts, the police could not stop what Boris had done. Only he knew where the device was located, and he would be out of the country soon. There was no going back. History had been written, and Boris was the author.

He smiled as he skipped up the road in a childish jaunt, knowing that in only a few hours, he would get to kill so many Americans.

He was completely untouchable and impossible to stop.

Chapter 28

Jacob sat across from Kramer Kay, reeling from what she told them.

"Hold up," he said. "So this blueprint thing the woman in the hospital said was true?"

"Yes," Kramer said. "We examine what we want to—or need to—learn from this incarnation and write a blueprint to that effect, similar to writing a book of your story on Earth, on this plane. We meet with our loved ones on the other side first and write it out with them so when we get here they can play their roles to make sure we go through what we came here to go through. All the while, they're doing the same with their blueprints."

"And we do this, why?"

"To evolve our souls. To become more worthy entities on the other side. Our blueprints are approved, and off we go to the parents we chose to help us start our lives here. Something you must consider. If we were to stay in Heaven

—let's call it that for want of a better word, but it's really the other side—it would always be magical and lovely. There's no learning, no molding up there. We come to Earth to learn, evolve, go through things, and become better individuals and souls."

Maria cut in. "So why would people commit suicide? I mean, if they wrote their own book before coming here, why write that little part?"

"In our blueprints, we often push ourselves too hard, asking for more than we can handle. A noble ambition as the idea is to evolve faster, but when we get here, we realize it's too much to handle, and we go home earlier than we should, which is akin to breaking your contract. Suicides end up having to come back and do it all over again until they get it right."

"This is a lot to take in," Jacob said. He rubbed his face, then met Kramer's gaze. "So why would Lance write a blueprint only to come here and be killed at ten years of age?"

"There's a reason, but it may be hard to hear."

"Try me."

"At first, it may even be hard to understand, but try to be open to it." Kramer paused, staring at Jacob. Then she nodded and began talking. "He chose his path to help you with your blueprint. In your previous incarnations here, you have never lost a child. So, you asked your best friend on the other side if he would come and spend ten years with you and then go home so you could try to learn to deal with the unique grief involved with such a loss. But there was another reason, too."

Jacob wiped a tear and motioned for her to continue. "This oughta be good."

"His passing sparked an anger in you that caused you to be relentless in finding his killers. The men who killed your son were contracted to kill you that day, which I think you may have figured out already. What you did because of Lance's death was go after and stay close to the murderers the whole time. They felt threatened by you, and that's why they tried to kill you again. Your job in the next twenty-four hours was written long before you came here, and it was intended to save thousands of people's lives. You wrote it, and you will fulfill it."

"And what is that? What is my job?" Jacob had an even harder time swallowing that he'd agreed that Lance would die at such an early age so that Jacob could evolve his soul from the learning experience of losing his son. Didn't sound so plausible. In fact, it sounded like madness and torture.

"Look, I need you to trust me. You don't have to believe me or alter your faith. Just trust me. From where I'm sitting, if everything I have said is true, we can still do something about this bomb that'll blow soon."

Maria jumped up from the table so suddenly that she startled Jacob. She moved into the corner to sob quietly.

"Maria?" Jacob whispered. "You okay?"

After a moment, he rose from his chair and went to her, wrapping an arm around her shoulder.

Maria turned to Kramer. "If what you're saying is true, then why did my husband have to die? So I could learn to deal with the grief? Is that what you're saying?"

Kramer nodded. "I'm sorry."

"This is bullshit," Maria said.

Jacob heard it first. A soft, melodic voice echoed throughout the kitchen. Maria stiffened in his arms.

"It is true," a male voice echoed in the room. "I'm so sorry, my love, but this is your path, your choice as well as mine."

Maria spun around, eyes wide. "John?"

"Be careful," Kramer said. "The first time this happens can be quite emotional and scary. Overwhelming, too. Are you okay, Maria?"

Maria nodded vigorously. She started for the entrance to the kitchen.

"He's coming toward us. You don't have to leave the kitchen."

Maria stopped and looked down at Kramer, then sat at the table.

Jacob watched the entrance to the kitchen, where the hall led down to what he thought would be the bedrooms.

"I'm sorry for scaring you earlier," the man whispered again. "That wasn't my intention."

"Can I see you?" Maria asked. "Are you here?"

"Yes."

There was movement by the door. Then, a shoulder appeared. To Jacob, it looked like it shimmered. A body formed in the doorway, then became more solid to the eye until a man glided into the kitchen like he was floating.

Maria jumped from her chair.

"Careful—" Kramer snapped.

Maria lunged forward and tried to touch the man. Jacob watched as her hand went through the image. It was like watching someone try to touch a holographic image.

"John, is it really you?"

"Yes, Maria, but only for a short time. It takes considerable energy to visit this plane, and even then, only a select few can ever see or hear us. You have the ability for now, but it'll wear off in the next few days as the effects of that accident by the river fade away."

Maria crossed herself. "Was that you earlier?"

"Yes. I often come at night and watch over you."

"Why didn't you say anything?" Maria asked.

"I was afraid I'd startle you, and I was still unsure if you could see me or not. You confirmed it when you ran from the house."

Jacob's heart was racing. He couldn't believe what he was seeing. All the faith in the world couldn't compete with this kind of proof. As he watched Maria reunite with her husband, he couldn't help but think of Lance and whether he would show up or not.

"Maria, listen, I can't stay. I need you to do what Kramer asks and work with Detective Jacob. He's the only one who can potentially stop this thing, but he needs your help. Will you do that?"

Maria nodded. "Of course, John. But when can I be with you?"

"Soon." John began to fade. "Soon. It's not your time yet, but soon. I'll be waiting for you, my love. Remember the heart and the arrow. You've got mine sewn up, my lovely."

And then he was gone.

Maria reached for the tissues and sobbed into them for a moment.

"You okay?" Kramer asked. "Should we continue?"

"Yes, please," Maria said.

"I assure you, there is no pain on the other side. There's only bliss. We come here, learn what we need to evolve and better appreciate our home, and then we go back. The real death is leaving the other side to come here. Then we are born when we return home to the other side."

Jacob leaned forward. "Will I see Lance?"

"Of course. He's been here the whole time. He's quite the strong little entity."

Jacob looked around the kitchen just as a Frisbee flew past him.

"Missed it, Dad."

Jacob grabbed the table to hold himself up. Kramer was talking. Her voice stabilized him as he leaned into the counter.

"Lance, buddy. What ..." Jacob braced himself with the table, his legs visibly shaking now.

"I'm good, Dad, but you gotta stop these guys."

"I will, son. I will."

"We can't tell you much except that they have a device, and it's intended to go off sometime tomorrow morning."

"Anything else?" He couldn't believe his son was standing before him, talking to him like nothing happened a year ago. And here he was, questioning his son about suspects.

"Just that it's downtown somewhere."

"You're on the other side. You can't be more specific?"

"No, because they have their own plans to live by as well. We aren't God. We don't know everything. You have to figure it out, and you need Steve, too. Please get him."

"Okay, Lance, I will."

"I can tell you that everyone who worked on this device is already dead except the man in charge. Something went wrong, and he killed the rest of his people. They're over here now."

"Over there? Are you safe?"

"Yes, silly. There is no Hell. That's a fable humans make up to scare others and use guilt to control them. There's here, and then there's where you are. That's it. Now, I gotta go. Get a couple hours' sleep, Dad, then go stop these people, okay?"

"Sure, Lance, I can do that." He felt like he was dreaming, in a daze while awake. "I'll see you soon."

Lance faded before his eyes, and then he was gone. Jacob glanced around and then back to where Lance had been shimmering. He was gone. Jacob turned back to Kramer and Maria.

"Uhm, words can't explain what just happened to us all."

"Now you can understand what my life is like. These entities are in my life every day, whispering their loved ones' names in hopes I can send messages to ease their grief. Which is why I do it because I'd go mad keeping these voices to myself.'"

Jacob laughed. "You hear voices and repeat what they say to others to avoid madness. Maybe that's the cure for schizophrenia."

"I don't know why you two need Steven Wallace, but I'm told you do. Somehow, I understand Mr. Wallace is pivotal."

"We can get Steve. But shouldn't I alert someone that there's a bomb downtown? I mean, should I follow the routine on this?"

"No, because you don't know who's compromised. If your own boss was in on it and tried to kill you, I'm not sure that's a good idea."

They talked for another hour. Drowsy after all they'd been through, the trio wound down with plans to wake at six in the morning to go and break Steve out of the hospital.

Jacob lay on the couch, the lights out, his mind racing, knowing he would do everything to find this bomb and he would diffuse it or die trying because he wasn't afraid of death anymore.

In fact, death would be preferred so he could be with Lance.

Maybe that would be his end goal.

After speaking with the other side, he saw that being murdered had its advantages.

Chapter 29

"Jacob. Wake up. It's time."

He woke, leaving behind dreams of Lance playing with his mother. They were a family again. Loving one another, laughing with each other. The nightmare was when his eyes opened, and he was awake.

"I'm up," he mumbled. "What time is it?"

"It's six in the morning. We haven't much time."

Jacob leaned up, moaned, then swiveled his legs to sit on the edge of the couch. He rubbed his face and squinted at the bright light peeking through the living room curtains.

"How much time do we have? Do you know when the device will detonate?"

"No, but I was told it'll happen before noon." She stared at him, a somber expression on her face. "I'm beginning to worry we won't be able to stop this thing."

He watched her as she moved into the kitchen, where she slipped a spoon into a cup and stirred it.

Jacob shrugged, then yawned. "All we can do is pursue it like we've been asked to. They have faith in us." He glanced around the living room but didn't see any floating spirits. Was it all part of a dream? Or did he actually speak with his dead son hours ago?

"All we know is that there's a bomb downtown, and it's going to explode within five to six hours. This is so scary for me." She stepped to the kitchen door, a coffee cup in her hands. "I usually only deal with people asking to talk to dead loved ones. Not terrorists with bombs and shit."

"That's where I come in, I guess. Although I have little experience with terrorists, I go after criminals for a career."

"Good morning," Maria muttered as she came down the hallway from the bedrooms. "Did all that actually happen last night?"

Kramer nodded and sipped her coffee.

"So, are we ready to go fight crime?" She smiled, then let it drop. "I need a coffee."

Kramer pointed at the mugs on the counter. Jacob pushed up off the couch to have one, too.

"You sound happy this morning," Kramer said.

"After seeing my husband and knowing I can join him if everything goes to shit, I'm quite happy. Now, let's talk about that guy, Steve."

Jacob nodded. "Give me time for coffee. Then we'll leave and go get him."

***

The clock on the dash of Kramer's car said 7:18 a.m.

when they pulled up to the hospital.

"Okay, you know what to do, right?" Jacob asked.

"Yes." Maria nodded.

"Then let's go. No time to waste."

Jacob led Maria into the hospital while Kramer waited in the car. They took the elevator to Steve's floor and headed to his room.

Jacob was the first to notice that the cop outside Steve's room wasn't there.

"I wonder if he's in another room." Then he had another thought. "They had better not have moved him back to the facility or a holding cell."

A heavy-set woman sat alone behind the desk at the nurses' station.

"Can I help you?" she asked.

"I'm Detective Bryce Jacob. I was the police officer brought in when Steven Wallace was here, too. Can you tell me what room they moved him to?"

"He wasn't moved to another room. They checked him out. As far as I know, Mr. Wallace was taken to jail."

Jacob slammed a fist into his open hand. "Shit."

He turned to Maria. "Come on, we've got to hurry."

The woman muttered something, but Jacob was already running away and didn't hear what she said.

They ran out to the car and got in. "Kramer, take us to my detachment."

"What? Why?"

"They've checked Wallace out already. They're probably holding him until new charges are filed. Once that happens, he'll get a bail hearing. He could be at the bail hearing this morning if they were fast enough, which would pose problems for us."

"Tell me why he's so important again?" Maria asked from the back seat as Kramer pulled out of the hospital parking area.

"I have no idea," Kramer said. "All I know is you two need him. That's the information I received."

"They couldn't be more specific?" Jacob asked.

She chortled. "That's just a glimpse of some of the difficulties I have to work with daily."

When the trio pulled up in front of the police station, Jacob hopped out. "You two stay here and be ready. We may be in a hurry when I come out with Steve." He turned away but then stopped and turned back. "If I need support from the other side, can I just ask? I mean, how does this work?"

"As far as I know, you can. I mean, you're in touch with it now." She shrugged. "It works differently for everyone."

Jacob nodded. "Got it, thanks. I may need to try something in there."

He bolted from the car, hit the stairs running, pushed through the front doors, and headed for the holding cells. It was almost eight in the morning, and they didn't have Wallace with them. He felt the sand slipping through the hourglass, the proverbial timer, and the top almost empty.

No one interrupted him on his way to the holding cells. One friend nodded his way and said he was glad to see him back in the building, but that was it. A couple of officers loyal to McGregor, who had no idea what actually happened, scowled at him as he ran by.

Fred Martin sat at one of the desks closest to the holding

cells. Martin had been there for as long as Jacob could remember.

"Hey Martin, I gotta see Steven Wallace. Which cell is he in?"

Martin glanced up and frowned. "Number three, but you can't go in there."

Jacob stared back at him. "Why not? I'm his arresting officer."

"I know, but it's in the report."

"What report?" He shook his head. "Wait, I don't care about any reports. Just open the door so I can access his holding cell. I need to speak with him."

"There are orders not to let anybody near him."

Jacob moved closer to Martin. "Look, open the damn door. I haven't much time and need to speak to Wallace."

"Are you even on duty?" Martin leaned back in his chair and crossed his arms. "Didn't McGregor suspend you before you killed him?"

Jacob stared at him a moment, then moved over to grab a chair from another desk. He plopped down beside Martin, moving inside the man's comfort zone.

"What are you doing?"

"I need you to listen to me."

"I am listening, and the answer is still no fucking way."

Jacob glanced around to see if his son or that woman from the hospital was floating close by, but there'd be no help from the other side on this one.

"No one is here to help you," Martin said, then laughed.

Jacob was done listening, and he was done playing nice.

He planted his feet, leaned forward, and then punched

Martin in his gut. As the man leaned forward, he delivered an uppercut to the face.

Jacob grabbed the man's collar and yanked him back into a seating position.

"Keep your whining down," Jacob whispered through his teeth. "I'm so done fucking around." He slipped a hand inside Martin's jacket, yanked out his service weapon, and placed it against Martin's knee. "Get the fucking keys and escort me to Wallace."

Jacob peered over Martin's shoulders, but of the few officers in this area, no one paid them any attention.

"Fuck you," Martin mumbled, blood dripping from his mouth. He must've bitten his tongue.

Jacob pressed the weapon against Martin's kneecap. "I just killed the sergeant, and you're telling me you want to join him."

Martin shot a glance at the gun, then back into Jacob's face.

"Okay, fuck you, Jacob. I'll get you your boy, but you're dead."

"Sounds good to me."

Martin glared at him a moment longer.

"Now." Jacob jerked his head toward the holding cells.

Martin fumbled with something in his desk, and then they got up together and moved toward the corridor where the holding cells were lined up.

Jacob followed Martin inside, the door closing behind them. He eased away from Martin, the gun held by his pant leg. They were isolated in the hallway, and as far as Jacob could tell, no one had noticed their skirmish. Cameras above them might detect something, though. He had to get in and get out if he had a chance of ever leaving this place today.

"Whatever you're planning is stupid," Martin said. "You're in a building filled with cops. This is the worst place to do something like this. You know you won't get out of here."

"Watch me."

Jacob walked backward until he saw Wallace.

"Open the door." He tapped the gun at his side to remind Martin who was in control.

Once he heard the clicking sound, he pushed on the door. Steve lay on his back, staring at the ceiling.

"Get up. We have to leave. Come on."

Steve spun toward him. "Man, am I glad to see you, which is something I never thought I'd ever say. Someone visited me last night and said there's some kind of bomb in the city."

Jacob was amazed, but it made sense. Wallace could see and hear the other side as much as they could.

"There is, and we're going to find it."

"Well, we won't have to look too hard."

Jacob had no idea what the junkie was talking about but pushed him toward Martin and the exit door.

"Why won't we have to look too hard?"

"Because I think I know where it is."

Jacob bumped into Martin and shoved him to the floor. "Give me the keys."

Martin handed them to him. "You're dead meat."

"Fuck you, Martin."

Jacob peeked out the door and saw no one in the area.

They still weren't home-free but could potentially be out of the building in minutes if all went well.

He looked back at Steve. "How could you know something like that? Where is it?"

"Well, I don't exactly know. Get me downtown, and I'll be able to tell you."

Jacob frowned. "How does that work?"

"My visitor called it psychic location something or other. I'll just feel it as we close in. They'll help me." Wallace waved an arm in a circle as if pointing at others around him.

"You guys are so ready for the looney bin," Martin said from the floor as he wiped blood from the side of his mouth.

"Sorry, mate," Jacob said. "Can't have you raising the alarm. Too many people to save today to worry about one cop losing consciousness."

"What? I'm not losing anything—"

Jacob drove a fist into the side of Martin's head so hard that the man's head bounced once off the concrete floor, and his eyes rolled back in his head. Fred Martin slouched over, completely unconscious.

"Damn, didn't know I could do that with one solid hit." Jacob grabbed the door knob. "Wallace, we'll talk more on the way. First, we have to get out of here."

Jacob checked that the safety was on, slipped the weapon into his pants, and stepped out into the main area. It remained relatively empty. He motioned for Steve to follow.

"Listen, we could encounter resistance along the way, so just follow my lead."

"Aren't you a cop? Don't you work here? Why would they stop you?"

"Well, I stole a gun, and I'm not on duty. Me and a fellow officer killed our sergeant, and I just knocked another cop out."

"You know, Detective Jacob, you're all right."

Jacob moved forward with Wallace in tow. This was too easy, but there was no other way out. He had to leave the way he had come.

He placed a finger over his lips for Wallace to remain quiet, then started for the stairs that led up one level. They reached the door and entered the stairs without meeting resistance.

Once in the stairwell, they hit the stairs running.

"Freeze!" someone shouted from the level above.

Jacob stopped, and Wallace bumped into him. His hand wrapped around the butt of Martin's weapon, but at the same time, he saw his son about five feet from him, shaking his head back and forth.

"Drop it!" the man shouted.

Jacob glanced higher and was dismayed to see at least twenty police officers lined along the railing, their guns drawn and all aimed at him and Wallace. When he looked over at his son, Lance was disappearing again.

"Is that really necessary?" Jacob asked. "All those guns for me?"

Richard Cranston stepped away from the armed wall of men and stepped down two stairs before stopping. "I want every gun trained on Detective Jacob until he drops the weapon he has stashed in his pants."

Jacob knew the drill. There was no time to negotiate, nor was there room. They had him—no doubt. He bent over slowly and set the gun on the stairs, then softly kicked it away. The weapon clanged down several more stairs before stopping on the level below.

"Good," Cranston said, then descended the stairs toward Jacob. He moved past him and bent to retrieve the gun, made sure the safety was on, and then turned to the officers above them, motioning with his arm for them to put their guns away. "Everyone back to work. The show is over."

"We gotta leave, Sergeant," Jacob said. "Like, now."

He shook his head. "No one is leaving this building." He eyed him with one eyebrow raised. "What happened to you, Jacob? All those reports that you're losing it. McGregor was about to suspend you, and he's killed in your hospital room while allegedly trying to *kill* you. And now you're in your own police station, breaking out prisoners and beating fellow officers. What's going on, man? Tell me you've gone crazy so I can feel sorry for the mental issues you're dealing with. Please, give me something to work with here."

"I can explain everything tomorrow, but I don't have time today. You have to listen to me. Someone is going to blow up a large part of Los Angeles sometime this morning, and I have to stop it."

"Oh really? And aliens are coming to abduct the Queen of England, too, right? Tell me, are you fucking mad?" He motioned with Martin's gun in his hand. "Start walking. You can tell me all about it once you're locked up in a jail cell pending your arraignment tomorrow morning."

Chapter 30

He couldn't handle it anymore.

A madman never doubts his sanity. Boris repeated this mantra to himself repeatedly, but it wasn't working. He was going crazy with the waiting, and it didn't help that he was overtired.

A quick look at his watch, and it was twenty minutes to nine. His plane would be boarding after ten. He still had over an hour and a half to lounge around the airport. People watched him. He could feel it. Airport security had been by twice already. That wasn't routine, was it?

The woman across from him had two little boys running around, acting like undisciplined fools. The man sitting three seats from Boris was reading a newspaper. But was he really reading it, or was he watching Boris, waiting for him to pull out the cell phone detonator?

Boris decided to take a walk.

He got up, gathered his carry-on, pulled out the handle to

drag the case, and turned toward the aisle. One of the two boys ran right in front of him. He almost tripped over the small punk.

"I'm sorry ..." the boy whispered, running away laughing.

Boris looked at their mother.

She smiled at him. "They got a lotta energy. Don't mind 'em."

The woman had an accent Boris couldn't place. Whatever it was, her voice came out, making her sound stupid. If a voice could measure intelligence, this woman's certainly did.

"Don't worry, I won't."

He left her watching him, probably wondering what he meant.

People were gathering in different areas. Men, women, and children all traveled to other regions of the globe, all safe from him and his bomb. He looked from face to face as he walked, guessing if he could measure how stupid they were.

That's when he noticed people were watching him again. But that couldn't be. No one knew who he was or what he was doing. The people who knew about him had no idea where he was.

Boris moved faster. It was time to find a restaurant or coffee shop near the back of the airport, away from his gate, so that no one could monitor him.

He passed an entire row of gates and traversed long walkways until he reached a small cafeteria-style sandwich shop in a corner between doors that led to a shopping area. A seat at the back was empty. Boris purchased a coffee and moved to the rear of the cafeteria.

He sat and scanned the immediate area. No hostiles in sight. He shook his head and wiped his face. Moisture covered his hand. He was sweating and raising his own blood pressure. What was wrong? What was bothering him? Killing people was never a problem. Killing hundreds at once was fine with him. These people were his enemy.

So then, why was he freaked out? Because he came this close to ending his mission here, and he wasn't home free yet?

He grabbed the side of the table and tightened his grip. He was determined to see it through. Nothing would stop him. No one in that airport knew who he was or his purpose. In fact, he'd already cleared security.

"Are you all right, sir?" A man approached his table.

Airport security.

"I'm fine."

"You don't look so good, sir. Can I get someone for you?"

"No, no, I'm fine." Boris smiled. He lowered his head. "I'm sorry. I don't like to fly. I always take the train." He looked back at the officer. "But I will be okay. Business has called me to Europe, and I can't take the train there, so I will deal with it."

The guard smiled in a consoling effort. "It's okay. I see this every day. You're not the only one. These big birds are safe, though. I assure you, there's nothing to worry about."

"Okay, thank you."

The guard stepped away and left him alone.

"Get control of yourself," Boris whispered under his

breath.

He pulled out the cell phone. Maybe he should just blow it now. That way, no one would be able to stop him.

The number was preprogrammed. Hit send twice, and the call would send the signal, and that would be it. Three minutes later, massive damage at the Department of Water and Power and surrounding buildings. Hundreds, if not thousands, would be killed.

His thumb hovered over the send button. He waited a heartbeat, then another. He lowered his thumb to push the button once. The phone lit up. The number appeared on the screen.

One more hit, and it would be done.

Fuck it.

He hit send again.

There was three minutes left.

Chapter 31

"SERGEANT CRANSTON, YOU'RE NOT LISTENING. WHAT happened out there two weeks ago caused something to happen in our heads—"

"That's enough!" Cranston slammed his hand on the table, stopping the recorder. "I can't tape any more of this shit. Are you fucking serious?"

Jacob looked at Wallace and then back to the acting sergeant. "Absolutely."

"You want to go on record with this statement? Okay, fine with me, but that means your career is over. I will have you committed for an involuntary assessment. That's seventy-two hours of testing to see how crazy you really are." The acting sergeant leaned forward. "You've really lost it, my friend."

Jacob clasped his hands together on the table. The three of them had been in the room for ten minutes, and nothing had been achieved. They were running out of time. The chance of stopping the men who killed Lance was slipping away. There was literally no time left. At most, he had maybe two hours to find a bomb somewhere in downtown Los Angeles. He had failed. There was no way around it. Being locked inside an interrogation room of a police station was getting him nowhere. Telling Sergeant Cranston the truth had made things worse.

Jacob wondered why they had to come and get Wallace if that led to both of them being held and no one was looking for the bomb. How long would Kramer and Maria wait out front for them, too?

"Cranston, listen to me."

"No, I've had enough of this stupid shit. I respected you coming up through the ranks. I remember how you used to always say earn and honor rank. I know a few of the guys don't like you, but shit, we all have those. Last year, when you lost your son, the Jacob I knew died with him, too. Everyone saw it."

"Cranston. Listen. To. Me." Jacob was at the edge. There had to be a way out of this. There just had to be. He glared at Cranston, all the intensity and emotion on his face. "There is a bomb in Los Angeles."

"I know. We covered that—"

"No!" Jacob yelled. "Shut up and listen." He felt Wallace lean away from him. "I can stop this thing from happening. It's a consortium of some kind. They built this bomb and tested a version of it in the river at the Amy Greg Center. Forget for a minute what I said about it changing the three of us and focus on the case. McGregor was working with them. I was getting close to them a year ago, and they tried to take me out. Instead, they killed Lance, figuring it would slow me down. These are the kinds of people I'm talking about. They would kill a child. Why else was McGregor in my hospital room with a gun? Why would he shoot Everton?"

Someone knocked on the door.

"Enter," Cranston shouted, his face reddening while listening to Jacob.

The door opened, and an officer stuck his head in. "You wanted a report as soon as we had ballistics."

"I'm busy right now, but go ahead."

The officer nodded. "Well, ballistic reports confirm Detective Jacob's story about the shooting last night. The men he killed were identified as Russian. They were heavily armed. And Detective Jacob, your car is totaled."

"It's okay," Jacob said. "It's insured."

"Leave us." Cranston waved his hand to shut the door.

The officer pulled back and shut the door.

"They were the same people who kidnapped that scientist, Dan Morgan, and his wife. I was meeting with McGregor when he asked the homicide detective on the Morgan case if Morgan could be used to help build a bomb."

Cranston cocked his head. "How do you know about all that? From one meeting in McGregor's office?"

"Homicide briefed McGregor on it when I was in a meeting with him the day he ordered me to go to the Amy Greg Center."

Wallace fidgeted beside Jacob, probably getting antsy for a fix while knowing the clock was ticking.

Cranston tapped the table with his fingers. "Funny you should mention it. Morgan was picked up last night wandering the streets. He kept saying they killed his wife. It took us hours to locate where they were holding him. We can't get in until we get a warrant, which is being drawn up this morning. When I leave here, I'm going to—"

"Wait, don't tell me. Giotech Pharmaceuticals."

Cranston's eyes widened for a brief moment, but Jacob caught it.

"How did you know? Is this tied to an ongoing case or something?"

"They were the ones I investigated a year ago. It's all in the report I dropped off to McGregor the weekend Lance was killed."

Cranston drummed his fingers on the table again while staring at Jacob. "Since we're talking and not shouting, can I press record again?"

"Of course, but we're out of time. We must do something about this device downtown, and we have to act now."

"Jacob, if the Russians had a bomb, wouldn't the NSA or the FBI know about it? They monitor chatter for this kind of thing. Besides, why else would they kidnap Morgan if not to help them with such a device." Cranston shrugged. "He hasn't mentioned anything about it."

"At this point, I don't care why they kidnapped Morgan. Maybe they had Morgan working on a piece of the device, and that by itself didn't resemble a threat to Morgan. Look, Cranston, Wallace, and I need to leave here, or this bomb will go off, and all the dead will be on your hands. Although, my sources are telling me that I may be too late already. We may not be able to stop it."

"Well, if you're hearing you can't stop it," he smiled,

"stick around so we can talk more."

"You're not listening." Jacob leaned forward. "We need to leave. Now."

Cranston leaned in closer to Jacob. His boss's breath was sour.

"You're not listening, Detective Jacob. You're not going anywhere. Are we clear?"

Jacob detected movement over Cranston's shoulder. Lance materialized, then whispered something.

"What?" Jacob said, staring at the image of his son.

"I said, you're not going anywhere—"

"Not you," Jacob barked at Cranston. "My son is standing right there."

Cranston spun around, then back to Jacob, glaring at him.

Lance spoke again. "Tell him his mother is here to see him."

Cranston got to his feet and reached for the door. When he knocked to have it opened, Jacob faced him.

"Richy Rich, turn around. You have some explaining to do."

Cranston stood by the door, head slightly bowed. Then, in an almost imperceptible tone, he said, "My mother used to say that." He lifted his head and looked at Jacob. "Where did you hear those words?"

The door opened, and Cranston waved them off. "We'll be a few more minutes."

He reclaimed his seat across from Jacob. "You were about to tell me where you heard that."

"Your mother, Silvia, is here. She came to talk sense into you." Jacob lifted his hands in defense. "Her words."

Chapter 32

The call didn't go through. But that was impossible.

Boris checked the signal strength. No bars were evident. The back corner of the cafeteria was shielded by enough concrete that his phone couldn't get a strong enough signal.

"Fuck," he cursed under his breath.

This onset of his recent paranoia wouldn't stop him. In fact, nothing would stop him.

He sipped his coffee, leaned back in the uncomfortable restaurant chair, and waited. The plan would work. He would stick to the plan. As soon as he was airborne, he would call the bomb. Acquiring cellular reception from a few feet off the ground would be no problem. Then he'd place it in airplane mode, and that would be the end of it.

Yet something still nagged him. Was it that meddling Detective Jacob? Could that asshole still be bothering him? There was no way Jacob could stop the mission now. Not with the cell phone in Boris's hand. If there were any sign of trouble, Boris would detonate. That was it. There were no takebacks.

So then, what was there to worry about?

With a long pull from his coffee, Boris finished it and rose from his seat. Agitated as he was, he couldn't sit still. What if they were mobilizing against him right now? He sat in a corner with nowhere to run. He was leaving himself open without an escape route.

That was stupid.

He pulled the carry-on behind him and casually strode back into the main corridor, blending in with other travelers lounging near their various gates.

A clock hanging from the ceiling read 9:10 a.m.

It was almost time.

Almost time.

Chapter 33

CRANSTON STARED AT JACOB AND WALLACE for half a minute, his mouth opening, then closing.

Finally, he said, "You've got my attention. Tell me something else."

Jacob closed his eyes and focused on the new voice he was hearing—a woman's voice.

He opened his eyes after a few moments and met Cranston's gaze.

"She wants me to convince you it's her."

"How will she do that?" The redness in Cranston's face from earlier was gone. The man had blanched.

"She explained that … oh, wait." Jacob stopped and cocked an ear. "This is difficult as I'm new to it. Give me a second." He closed his eyes again. "Okay, she's back. She said you're a Taurus. She told me to convince you because you were a stubborn kid."

"You said that." Skepticism laced his words. Cranston

started tapping on the table again.

"Stop doing that." Jacob pointed at the man's fingers. "I can't concentrate. Now, ask me anything."

Cranston placed his hands on the table, palms down. "Ask what?"

"Whatever you want to verify, I'm talking to your mother."

Cranston got up from his chair and spun in a circle, looking exasperated. "I can't believe we're even doing this. How do you pull me into this shit, Detective Jacob? Do you know how crazy this is? I will *not* pretend to talk to my dead mother. She's been dead for—"

"Seven years," Jacob cut in. "I know. She just told me. She said she expected this kind of disbelief from you. It's how you lost Jenny."

Cranston stared down at Jacob. "How could you possibly know about Jenny? Have you been looking into my past?"

"Yes, Sergeant, absolutely. I investigated you for this very moment when I *knew* you would be detaining me, and I would need a way out because I have nothing else to do with my life." The sarcasm in his voice came easy. "Look, you haven't heard a thing I've said, have you? Come on, Cranston. This is serious. Ask a question so you can verify that I'm talking to your mother. Hurry, we're almost out of time. I can feel it."

Cranston stepped back and leaned against the wall, arms crossed over his chest. He stared at Wallace in the corner for a long moment. Jacob glanced over to see why. Wallace was watching the two of them, his eyes, mouth open.

"What?" Cranston asked.

"This is real," Wallace said. "I've heard it myself. If you listen to Jacob, you might save lives today."

"So, you're saying this thing that happened to Jacob happened to you too? For real?"

"Yes, and that woman as well."

Cranston fixed his attention back on Jacob. "And that was why you needed him? So you three superheroes could go out and save Los Angeles?"

"What time is it?" Jacob asked.

Cranston flipped his wrist and checked his watch. "9:12 a.m."

"This thing will be over by noon today, perhaps earlier. I'll have a full report on your desk about how I brought it to you, and you locked me down. My report will also go out to the FBI as this bomb was put there by the Russians."

"Are you threatening me or blaming me or both?"

"Cranston, I'm still attempting to convince you to listen to me."

The sergeant turned away and spoke with his back to Jacob. "What color was Jenny's bicycle in grade four?"

"What?"

"I asked a question. You wanted me to ask something, so I did."

"That sounds tough. They're not gods over there. They may have specific knowledge about you, but ... wait, she's saying something."

Cranston turned around and looked at Jacob.

"Red. She said it was red. How could she know that?"

"My mother taught fourth grade at Dillon Elementary. Jenny was in her class. We found out one Christmas when going through old photos. My mother used to help her unlock her bike every day after school because Jenny kept forgetting the combination."

"Are you convinced your mother's here yet?"

Cranston hesitated. "One more question. A color could've been a good guess. Tell me, what year did I buy my first car, and what kind of car was it? There's no way you could guess something like that."

Jacob listened and lifted his head to look at the ceiling tiles.

"It was April 1985. The car was a Buick Century Custom. Big green boat, she says. The previous owner was your mother. She sold it to you for eight hundred bucks. Are we in now?"

Cranston sat down hard. "How is this possible?"

"It is. Just accept it. Will you help us now?"

"My mother …" he stared at Jacob almost as if he wasn't seeing him. "Is she okay over there?"

"Of course. We'll talk more about that after we stop the bombers from detonating." Jacob cocked his ear again. "She's gone. She sends her love. She told me to say, don't be bitchy Richy. Something about that not being manlike. Now listen, we gotta move."

Cranston wiped his face and stood up. "Okay, let's roll. I'll grab Morgan as he's still giving his statement, and we'll head to Giotech Pharmaceuticals. Do you still need Wallace here? Might be hard getting him out of here."

"I'm being told that I don't need Wallace now. Apparently, his purpose was to get me here to speak with you."

Cranston opened the door and entered the hallway with Jacob on his heels.

"Speak with me?" Cranston said. "Seems like all I've done is hold you back."

"I need to enlist your help. I wouldn't have been able to do this without you, and I would never have asked for your help. I'm being told this worked out perfectly. I also hear there's still time, but we must move fast."

Cranston called over an officer and instructed him to escort Jacob upstairs, then take Wallace back to holding.

Jacob shook Wallace's hand. "Thanks for letting me handle that in there. You were mostly quiet the whole time."

Wallace nodded. "I was told to relax and wait. That it wasn't my time to die yet. So, I'm happy I'm staying behind."

"Good luck to you," Jacob said as if it was the last time they'd speak. Something told him they'd never see each other again.

"Meet me out front," Cranston said. "I won't be long."

Chapter 34

"HOW MUCH LONGER BEFORE WE GET there?" Jacob asked.

The clock on the dash of the undercover SUV read 9:40 a.m.

"We're five minutes out now," Cranston said. "I've got the warrant. The team behind me is forensics and extra men if we run into trouble." He glanced over at Morgan. "Your job is simple. Direct us as best you can to the elevator leading us to the basement where you said you were held. Can you do that?"

Morgan nodded.

He hadn't said much since they got in the vehicle. Outside the police station, Maria joined them, and they all took off toward Giotech with two loaded LAPD SUVs. Kramer Kay said she'd head downtown and see if she could get a read on where the bomb was located.

Jacob was told that no one had heard from Morgan's wife since his escape and that Morgan feared the worst. The guy was blaming himself even though his escape was heroic. Morgan and his wife—both of them—would be dead right now if Morgan hadn't escaped.

Cranston pulled the SUV onto the road that led to the Giotech Pharmaceuticals building. Smoke rose from an area near the fence line. Dozens of people were gathered around the front and walking throughout the parking lot.

"What's going on?" Jacob asked.

No one answered him as Cranston slowed to a stop by a barrel with a fire. Two men approached the SUV.

"Who're you guys?" the shorter one asked.

The man appeared to be in his forties.

"LAPD," Cranston said. "We have a warrant to search the premises. What's going on here? You guys on strike?"

"Nope," the man said. "Not really. We came to work this morning, and the building was locked down. A lawyer was here to hand out pink slips. I guess the company has gone under, but we decided to stay because they didn't pay us our final cheques."

"Is this lawyer here now?"

"No, he left a half hour ago. I think he was getting scared when everyone started to organize this protest. You ever heard of flash mobs?"

"Yeah, listen, who can get us in the building? Anyone here got a key?"

"Lorna over there does, but that big city lawyer said we'd be in trouble if we entered the building. He collected all the office staff's keys but not Lorna's."

"Why not Lorna's?"

The man leaned closer to Cranston's window. "She left

her laptop on her desk yesterday. She said she was waiting for the lawyer to leave so she could run in and get it. We don't get paid much. Can't leave that sort of thing behind. You understand?"

Cranston nodded and looked through the windshield. "Which one is Lorna?"

"She's the one in pink by the corner of the building …"

Cranston hit the gas and drove toward Lorna. People scattered, moving out of the way of the approaching SUV. Jacob turned around and saw the other SUV was right on their ass.

"Everyone out," Cranston ordered as the vehicle stopped.

"Lorna," Cranston shouted. "This here's a warrant to search the premises. I need access to this building immediately."

Lorna appeared to be stunned as she stood there shaking her head.

"Lorna, pull out your keys and give us access. Then lead us through to the basement."

Without glancing at the warrant, Lorna walked the ten steps to the main doors and produced a ring of keys. Within a minute, Cranston's team was inside and spreading out across the lobby of Giotech.

Jacob grabbed Maria and whispered for her to stay close. He looked everywhere but saw no movement. He was searching for anyone who might drop by from the other side to give them some direction.

Cranston was arguing with Lorna about the lower levels. Morgan stood there trying to explain how he was held captive below. Jacob moved toward the back of the building, with Maria following close behind. Just before he was out of earshot, he heard the woman asking if Morgan was the guy who attacked their boss on the fourth floor.

"I wonder what that's all about?" he said to Maria.

"I'm worried, Jacob. It's almost ten in the morning. We're running out of time and no closer to stopping this. Even if we do find a bomb, what are we to do with it?"

"I know, I know. My only consolation is they wouldn't have given us this knowledge if they didn't think we could do something about it."

"Okay, but what? And how?"

"I have no idea, but I learned something years ago. Once you have the *will*, the *how* reveals itself. So, since we're willing to do something, we just don't know how yet. It'll come. I have faith."

Images formed on the windows as they neared the back of the offices. The shape of a head formed on a window. The movement caught his eye and drew him closer.

"Maria, come here. Look at this."

Maria moved so close to him that she bumped his arm. It made him feel good, alive. Someone needed him and relied on him. Someone wanted his protection.

"It's Lance," Jacob whispered. "What's going on, son? Why can't you form stronger like before?"

"You're losing the ability. To see me. And to hear us. It was always … a temporary thing. It's fading now."

"Then hurry. Tell us—" He stopped talking as another form evolved on the window. Maria's husband's face shone through. They looked like faint clouds moving in the breeze.

"Maria, are you seeing this?"

"Not really, but I can hear a distant voice. What are they saying?"

Jacob leaned closer. Already, the images were fading. Lance moved his lips, but Jacob couldn't hear him anymore.

"I can't hear you," Jacob shouted. "Tell us what to do."

Only one word came through. *Hope.*

"Great, that helps. Don't worry about it. We have hope. But I think we need more to go on."

The images waned and then faded until Jacob looked through the glass at the pavement of the back parking lot below.

"Damn. We need Kramer Kay. There's no way we can do this without her. I need to be able to talk to Lance and John and whoever else wants to tell us shit."

Pounding footsteps drew his attention. He spun around to see Cranston running up to them.

"Let's go. We're out of here. I'm leaving a few men behind until the coroner gets here."

"Coroner?" Jacob asked. "What happened? What did you find?"

"Multiple bodies two levels below us. Also, I had two men go up to the offices on the fourth floor with Lorna to see if they could get a lead on where this guy was, and they found an itinerary for flights to Russia leaving Saturday."

"But it's not Saturday."

"Exactly. We think they upped the timetable because they knew Morgan would talk. Whoever's in charge executed the men working on the bomb and rebooked flights for today. We're heading to the airport with Lorna so she can ID the man she's calling Hector. Let's go."

As they ran toward the front of the building, Jacob said, "Cranston. You go with Lorna, and I'll drive the other SUV with Maria and Morgan. We need to go downtown and find Kramer and diffuse this device."

They hit the front doors running and exited into a small crowd of ex-employees who had gathered to stare out the windows.

At the SUVs, Cranston surprised him by grabbing his hand. He shook it and patted Jacob's shoulder. "Thanks," he said, then tossed him a set of keys, and they all hopped into their respective vehicles.

"What was that handshake all about?" Maria asked. "It looked like he was saying goodbye."

"Maybe he was." Jacob glanced over at her, then slammed the accelerator down. "Maybe he was."

Chapter 35

Boris waited until the women, children, and elderly entered the gates. Then, they began boarding the seats at the back of the plane. He'd requested seats near the emergency exit as insurance.

He checked the time and saw it was twenty-two minutes past ten in the morning. He'd be in the air in forty minutes. The bomb would detonate, and everything would be done. One final scan around the immediate area calmed him as no one was watching him. Not even a cursory glance his way. He'd been paranoid for no reason.

He pulled out the cell phone and powered it up to check for signal bars. Out here, in the middle of the waiting area surrounded by large windows, he had full signal strength. Two taps of the send button would be all it took. No one would even have the chance to get close to him.

The attendants called for all other passengers to begin boarding now. People throughout the waiting area got to their feet and formed a line.

Boris remained seated and waited, watching everyone.

The attendants were quick. Passports were checked and verified along with boarding passes. The line shortened. Gate C, with a direct flight to Moscow, which was just under thirteen hours, was emptying.

Boris rose and ambled toward the attendants, the cell phone in hand, intently watching all movement around him. Two airport security men emerged from a door to his left. He watched them but soon saw they had no interest in him. He continued forward, his finger pressing against the send button just in case he needed to push it quickly.

"Passport, please?" a female attendant asked warmly.

Boris pulled out his passport and handed it over. She slipped it through a machine, read her screen, and returned it after reading his boarding pass.

"Thank you. Enjoy your flight."

Boris nodded and moved toward the tunnel that led to his plane. He was going to get away clean. Nothing could stop him now. Morgan must not have convinced the authorities fast enough. They had no idea where he was or who he was. The plane would take off in half an hour.

He checked the cell again. Battery power was still full, and signal strength was full.

He wondered why he was so worried as he fell in behind the people bunching up at the plane's door.

What could possibly go wrong?

Chapter 36

JACOB HIT THE FLASHING LIGHTS AND raced along the Santa Monica Freeway, knowing they had lost too much time. He'd left Cranston ten minutes ago, knowing full well that Cranston had a faster way to the airport.

He smacked the steering wheel hard with his right hand. "Why the fuck did I go this way? We're behind the others by at least twenty minutes now."

Maria looked pretty ragged. He hadn't even considered what she would be going through from the kidnapping, the coma, then trying to help her kidnapper, and finally talking to her dead husband. He could only hope she kept it together until this was over.

"I'm sorry," Jacob said. "Are you okay?"

Maria nodded and averted her gaze to her lap. She fumbled with her fingernails as a tear formed in her eye.

"What are you thinking?" Jacob asked.

"Just that …"

"What?"

"If it's so nice on the other side and I could be with John, maybe I have nothing left to live for. Maybe I should just, you know, die."

"No, that's not the answer. I wish I could be with my son, but that's life."

"And death." Morgan piped in from the back seat.

Jacob turned and looked at Morgan.

"What?" Morgan said. "I lost my wife with all this shit."

"Okay, we all lost someone, but so has everyone else on this planet. What does that mean? We should all die to be with them? We grieve, find closure, and move on. At least we got to see our loved ones and know they're waiting for us when we go home. That's more than the rest of these lost souls around us can say." Jacob gestured at the cars they were passing.

His cell phone rang. He pulled it out and answered.

"Yeah?"

"It's Kramer. Have you talked to Lance in the last little while?"

"I saw him about twenty minutes ago. Why?"

"Did he say anything to you?" Kramer asked.

"All I could make out was the word *hope*. Does that mean anything other than the obvious?"

"Yes, it does. I keep hearing they told you the street name. John, Maria's husband, came by looking quite worried. For some reason, they aren't being helpful anymore. Like it's supposed to happen or something. It's almost like we missed our chance."

"Wait a minute. Hope Street is in downtown Los

Angeles. Could they be trying to guide us to Hope Street?"

"Could be. Where are you now?"

"We're on the Santa Monica Freeway. We're just coming up to Harbor Freeway."

"Okay, one sec …" Kramer trailed off. "Get off on Harbor and go north. Go down North Third Street and access Hope Street that way. Something tells me you'll find what you're looking for on Hope Street."

"Kramer, the Department of Water and Power is on Hope Street."

"Jacob, I've got two entities with me. They're both nodding."

"Okay, I'm on it."

"I'll see you there—"

Jacob cut her off as he hit the end and then called Cranston's cell.

"Where are you, Jacob?" Cranston said into the phone.

"Following a lead. Look, I think we might have credible information on where the bomb might be. We're ten minutes out."

"We're just pulling into the airport."

"I have a feeling the bomb is located somewhere on Hope Street by the Department of Water and Power."

"What are you going to do when you find it? You need the bomb squad?"

"That's why I'm calling you. Contact them and have them meet us on Hope Street. I've got Morgan with me, too." Jacob glanced at him in the mirror.

Morgan nodded.

"Okay, I gotta go. We're here. I'll inform the bomb squad

to meet you on Hope Street double time. If anything happens, let me know."

Jacob hung up.

It took seven minutes to get to Hope Street. Once he turned up Hope, he drove slowly, all three of them looking for anything unusual. Just past West First Street, Morgan pointed.

"There. That's a Giotech Pharmaceuticals van."

Jacob nodded and pulled up beside the van, parking slightly behind it. He jumped from the SUV and looked inside the windows, then tried the van's doors, but they were locked. Maria and Morgan were getting out and coming around to him.

"Morgan, look in the back of the SUV for a crowbar or something to break into this van."

Jacob did a complete circle check and looked under the vehicle. Nothing seemed amiss. Morgan moved up beside him with a crowbar. To avoid having the driver sit on glass if the car had to be moved, Jacob smashed the passenger window out with one blow. He dropped the bar to the ground, reached in, and unlocked the door. A black curtain separated the back from the front. He eased it aside and peered into the back.

"Morgan, I need you here with me."

The van adjusted slightly as Morgan stepped inside behind Jacob.

"Tell me what that is," Jacob said.

"That's the device they were working on. It's bigger than the one they tested in the river by the detox center."

"Can you do anything with it?"

"I'm not sure. Let me take a look." Morgan moved around Jacob and climbed into the back.

Jacob watched for a full minute as Morgan explored the bomb from the top to the bottom. He looked back at Jacob and shook his head.

"We may have a problem," Morgan whispered.

Jacob's stomach twisted. A full sweat had broken out all over his body. The realization hit him hard: they were inside a vehicle holding a large device that could blow at any time.

"No, there are no problems. We can't have any of those. Just tell me you can cut a wire or something. There are too many people around here."

"Jacob, I'm sorry." Morgan appeared truly worried. "They've set up a cell phone detonator. Whoever has the cell phone can push a button from anywhere to set this thing off. It could go at any second. They would have rigged anti-tampering sensors or something, too. I'm sorry, but this isn't my field of expertise. I specialize in shockwaves and decibel levels. Not bombs."

Jacob was shaking. "Just try something without blowing us up while I call to see when the bomb squad's arriving."

He stepped back out of the van and almost bumped into Maria. She was leaning by the door, a large smile on her face.

"Why do you look so happy?"

"Because I can feel my husband all around me. Unlike you, I'm looking forward to going home."

Chapter 37

Sergeant Richard Cranston, followed by Lorna, ran through the double doors at departures and found security waiting. He'd called ahead, and they mobilized near the three gates where airlines had flights loaded bound for Russia.

"Who's in charge here?" Cranston asked.

"I am. Name's Dirk Stone. All the Russian-bound gates are locked down, with one plane already boarded. They have instructions to hold where they are."

"Lead the way to that gate first. We check that plane, then go gate to gate after that."

Cranston and Lorna followed the gaggle of security officers toward the gates. They half ran, half walked through throngs of travelers until they slowed near gate C29. Cranston was happy he didn't have to tell Lorna what to do. He noticed she was scanning faces the whole time.

Stone's men were solid, too. One ran into the men's washrooms while the others moved through the crowds, going on the descriptions Lorna offered over the phone on the way to the airport.

"What happens if we can't locate this man?" Stone asked.

"That's not an option," Cranston said. "Just find him." He turned toward Lorna. "Anything?"

She shook her head. "Nothing. He may not even be here. There are other flights tonight or tomorrow, too."

"He's here. Call it a hunch. This guy closed his offices, and he's bolting because Morgan got away. No," Cranston shook his head, "he's fleeing now. He's here."

"Sir," Stone stepped up to Cranston. "We're ready to board the plane that's already loaded."

"Lorna, these men will walk you on board. Scan every face. If he's on that plane, we have to know."

Lorna nodded.

Cranston's phone rang. He grabbed it. "Yeah?"

"It's Jacob. We found the bomb."

"What? Oh, wow! Great fucking job. Can Morgan disable it?"

"Doesn't look like it. He said it's set up to be detonated by a cell phone. Whoever's behind it can call it at any time, and we're done for."

"Where are you?"

"On Hope Street, right in front of the Department of Water and Power."

"So it's on me to find this guy and get that detonation cell phone out of his hands."

"Yeah, looks that way. Morgan will do what he can, and the bomb squad is twenty minutes away, but we've done all we can here. Cranston, find the cell phone. That's all we got. Our best option."

"We haven't located him yet, but we're entering a plane now to see if he's boarded. Call me back if you get that thing turned off."

"Just find the guy. Being this close to a device this size messes with your sense of self-preservation. All we want to do is run, but yet we stay. So, hurry, Cranston."

"I'm on it." Cranston ended the call and ran after Stone as they entered the tunnel that led to the plane.

A flight attendant greeted them at the door. The security had Lorna step on and start down the aisles. The TSA officers and Cranston waited at the door, the curtain pulled shut, their hands on their weapons.

Lorna came back a moment later. "He's not in first class."

"Okay, head to economy."

They all moved to the curtains that separated economy from first class and waited again as Lorna moved forward into the economy. Stone peeked through the curtains to keep an eye on her.

Cranston held his cell phone in one hand in case Jacob called back with an update. Every second counted while he waited for Lorna to return.

A full two minutes later, Lorna stepped through the curtains. She shook her head.

"Nothing. I'm sorry. If Hector had been sitting on this plane, I would've seen him. I know his face."

"It's okay." Cranston tapped her shoulder. "Thank you for your help. Go with Stone and his men. I'll follow you out in a minute, and then this plane can be on its way."

They moved back into the tunnel and away from him, but he couldn't let it go. None of it made any sense.

He parted the curtains and started down through the aisles with only a description to go by. Lorna had worked with the man and seen him daily. She'd recognize him on the spot, so Cranston's chances of finding the man were much slimmer than hers.

Could Lorna be lying to them? What reason would she have to lie, though?

Cranston had every reason to believe that Hector—or Boris, according to Morgan—was in the airport. Why wouldn't he flee immediately?

Unless he had already left the country. But Cranston didn't think so because the bomb hadn't been detonated yet. Why call from the other side of the world when you were local? And why stick around once your cover was blown?

The next few planes heading to Russia weren't scheduled for almost six hours. This had to be the one—the probability said so.

He'd reached the end of the aisle without anyone catching his eye.

No furtive glance, no looking away quickly, no one acting suspicious. Nothing.

His phone rang again. He answered it from the back of the plane.

"It's Jacob. We have trouble."

"What?"

"There's nothing we can do. The bomb squad boys are still not here. Anything on your end?"

"Nothing here."

Something clicked on his left. The lavatory door was closed.

Were people allowed to use them when they were parked at a gate?

The little sign on the door said, *occupied*.

Someone was in the bathroom. Someone was hiding.

Cranston was close enough to the bathroom door that whoever was inside would've heard his side of the conversation.

From a distance, he heard Jacob talking.

Cranston had let the phone drop from his ear. He placed it back and whispered, "Jacob, I'm here. Listen to me. I'm going to leave the line open."

Without waiting for a reply, Cranston slipped the phone into his breast pocket and then knocked on the lavatory's door.

"Open up. Police. I'm Sergeant Cranston with the LAPD. You have to open this door."

There was no response from the other side of the door.

Cranston banged on it again. "Open up!" he shouted.

People in the seats near the lavatories got up and moved down the aisle away from him.

Good, they should, in case this got ugly.

He pulled his weapon from its holster.

"I'm going to ask one more time. Open this door. LAPD."

More people were getting out of their seats now and moving toward the front of the plane. Someone was working his way down the aisle toward him, jostling between passengers.

Dirk Stone was coming.

The *occupied* sign flipped off on the lavatory's door.

Cranston stepped back, his weapon raised. Jacob's voice came from his cell phone in his pocket, but he ignored it.

Dirk Stone moved closer, his weapon also drawn.

"Step out slowly. We have the door covered."

There was no response.

Cranston raised three fingers for Stone to see, then lowered one. He then lowered the second one.

Stone nodded his understanding.

When his last finger dropped, Cranston grabbed the handle and shoved the door into the open position.

"Hands where I can see them," he shouted, his weapon aimed at the man's chest.

The man inside the lavatory reminded Cranston of Boris Yeltsin, the first Russian president in the nineties. He was a large man with white hair and a huge face.

The man's hands were raised, but he was smiling like he had nothing to worry about.

A cell phone was in his right hand, the man's thumb hovering over the cell's screen.

Cranston heard Jacob shouting at him through the phone in his pocket.

"You don't want to shoot me," the man said, his accent hard when speaking English.

"Put your hands behind your head, stand, and exit the lavatory slowly."

"No," the man said. "I think I will sit here a little more. But don't shoot. A lot of people will die if you shoot me."

The man exuded arrogance. Cranston had no idea how deep this man's schemes had gone, but a lot of people were already dead—kids too—because of him. If there was ever a perp, Cranston had an urge to shoot, this was it.

"We're in charge here. Exit the lavatory with your hands behind your head, or we'll drag you out. That device on Hope Street won't be hurting anyone."

The man blinked twice, then frowned slightly.

"Yeah, that's right, Boris or Hector or whatever you call yourself. We know all about your device and your plans. It's over. You're finished. Now, come out and give me that cell phone."

"I'll stand now." Boris slowly rose to his full height, his hand shoulder height now, his head slightly bowed as the roof was too low for him to stand straight up. "If I push this button, Hope Street will disappear, and you will shoot me. This doesn't work for either of us. So, I propose a deal."

"A deal? No fucking way." Cranston's arms were shaking. He couldn't hold his weapon on the guy much longer.

"Get the plane in the air, and I will give you the cell phone. Leave no one on the plane but you, me, and the pilots. That way, I leave the country, and no one dies today."

"Never. The only deal you'll get is your life. Hand over the cell phone, and I'll spare it." Cranston lowered his weapon, knowing Stone had him covered, and stuck out his hand, palm up for the phone.

Jacob was still yelling something on the phone. The tinny sound was fast becoming maddening.

"Shut up for a minute, Jacob. We're dealing with

something here."

"Are you speaking with Detective Bryce Jacob?" Boris asked, sweat sliding down his face, making him blink it away. The man had turned as red as a pomegranate.

Was the Russian stalling for some reason? Why did he seem so calm?

Had he already decided to detonate and knew he was about to die? Was the device on Hope Street a ruse, and the Russian was actually carrying the device on his person somehow?

"Yes, it's Detective Jacob. Want to say hello?"

"Of course, but I've got my own phone." The Russian waved it in front of him. Then he held it to his ear. "Goodbye, Jacob."

Time slowed as Cranston saw the man jab the phone with his thumb several times. Cranston couldn't get his weapon up fast enough to stop him.

The phone dropped from the man's hand and clattered to the lavatory's floor.

Stone moved closer, his weapon trained on the suspect while Cranston pulled the phone from his pocket.

"… it's set, it's set—"

"What's set?" Cranston broke into Jacob's chant. "The device didn't blow. We're still talking."

"Morgan said it set. There's a timer, and it's counting down from three minutes. The van also turned on like it was set with a remote starter. Morgan said it was connected to the van's battery somehow." Jacob's voice grew more hysterical with each word. "Cranston, there's nothing we can do. We're so fucked."

Cranston wavered on his feet, bumping into the wall behind him. "Jacob, think of something." The phone slipped from his grip as sweat coated his palm. He stared at the smiling Russian without bending to retrieve his phone.

A heartbeat later, he pushed off the wall and aimed his weapon at Boris.

"Turn it off."

The Russian shook his head. "I cannot. Once set, there's nothing anyone can do. How do you say in America? Oops?"

"Stone, who's that coming down the aisle?"

When Dirk Stone snapped his head away and looked toward the front of the plane, Sergeant Cranston fired his weapon twice.

The Russian's head exploded in the confines of the lavatory, blood and brain matter coating the interior like wallpaper.

"He made to attack me," Cranston said when Stone turned back around. He glanced at the TSA man in charge. "Oops."

Stone nodded. "I saw it, too, sir."

Chapter 38

Bryce dropped the cell phone and jumped into the front seat.

"How much time is left?" he shouted back at Morgan.

"Two minutes, thirty-four seconds."

Maria was already sitting on the passenger side. She slammed her door closed as Bryce slammed down the gas pedal. The van shot forward before he could shove her out the door. Every second counted now for what he had planned. In the next two minutes, he would shove her out when he stopped, or she'd succeed in seeing her husband sooner than she expected.

He hit West First Street, barely missed clipping a jacked-up pickup truck, and took a right turn, the van almost lifting on two wheels.

"Morgan, shout out the countdown as I drive."

"Two minutes, five seconds. But Detective, where are you going? You can't possibly get this out of the city in that time."

"Think about it. Remember the last time they detonated a device like this one?"

"The river. Nothing really happened—"

"That's right."

Morgan leaned forward. "The water took away over ninety percent of the device's power. Anything under the water will be fucked, but little will happen to those on the surface."

"Exactly. And Echo Lake is a few miles from here. If we can get this thing underwater in less than two minutes, we have a chance of killing this thing."

"Dead in the water," Maria said.

Bryce shot her a glance. The woman looked positively happy with the thought she might die in two minutes.

Harbor Freeway passed overhead, and the Vista Hermosa Park sign appeared on the right.

"We're at one minute, forty-eight seconds. This is cutting it close."

Bryce jogged to the right and dropped onto Glendale Boulevard. A large transport truck was parked at the stop sign up ahead. Bryce laid on the horn, but as he got to the bottom of the ramp, there was no room to maneuver around the truck. Maybe he could wedge between the concrete on the left and the truck on the right. Wouldn't that minimize the explosion?

"Hold on," Bryce shouted as he jerked the wheel and aimed the van for the small opening on the left of the transport.

The mirrors snapped off, and metal and concrete

screamed in protest as the van wedged itself into the small space available. All three of them were jerked forward.

Then the van popped through, and they were out of the tight spot. Bryce had been sure they'd get stuck, but all he did was shove the van through to the other side with the forward momentum he had going in.

"How much time now?" he asked as he pushed the pedal down again.

"One and a half minutes."

"You okay?" he asked Maria.

She nodded. "Just get us to that body of water."

They raced up Glendale Boulevard through a red light with cars jamming on their brakes to avoid hitting them and got lucky with a green light on Court Street. After negotiating a red light on Cortez, they passed under the Hollywood Freeway Bridge when Bryce's cell phone rang.

"How much time now?" he shouted back to Morgan.

"Under one minute."

Bryce hit the cell button and placed it at his ear. "Yeah?"

"I'm sorry, Jacob," Kramer Kay said into the phone, her voice cracking with tears. "I was just told what you're doing."

"It's okay, Kramer. This is my blueprint, right? My plan here? I'm supposed to be doing this, so I am. We all are."

"I'm a mile behind you."

"That's too close," he shouted. "You must stay back in case we don't make it."

"Half a minute," Morgan shouted, his voice hysterical now.

Maria leaned forward in her seat. It looked like she was

praying.

"Stop following us," Bryce shouted. "We're out of time."

"It's okay, Bryce. The blast radius gets contained. I already saw the outcome. I'm not coming for that. I'm coming for you three."

Echo Lake came into view on the right.

Bryce dropped the phone without saying goodbye while he scanned the fence for a spot to ram it.

He also wanted some sort of ramp to get the van as far into the body of water as possible.

The fence ended, and a path surrounded by green grass started. Twenty feet away was a small concrete abutment.

Without delay, Bryce hit the horn, spun onto the grass, and pushed the accelerator to the floor, aiming the van for the abutment.

"Windows down, so this baby will sink fast. Morgan, open the back doors and jump."

"Just over a dozen seconds left," Morgan shouted as he moved away toward the back of the van.

"Maria!" he shouted. "Jump out onto the grass."

The woman didn't move.

They were out of time.

The van connected with the concrete lifted upward and spun in the air. Time seemed to stand still for Bryce as the world twisted upside down.

The van impacted with the water on an angle, with most of the roof caving in. Water sloshed over them and filled the open van rather quickly.

Bryce hit the dash and was scrunched up against it as the side of the door pushed on his shoulder.

The windshield smashed out, and glass coated his face and arms.

Then, water rushed over him as the van began to sink.

He heard screaming and wondered if it was Morgan, but it stopped when water filled his mouth.

Everything was lighter now that they were underwater. Bryce yanked on his shoulder and was able to dislodge it. He spun to the passenger seat, saw Maria staring at him, and grabbed her arm.

Then he pushed through the open windshield and drew her out with him. Eddies formed around them as the van descended quickly.

Why hadn't the device detonated already? Was all that a waste of time?

The water was murky, the depths dark. He had opened his eyes but only detected light coming from above.

With enormous willpower, he thrust upward, fighting the pull of the water, Maria in his grip.

The light drew closer.

***

Bryce opened his eyes. Watcr lapped around him when he looked up. Maria and Morgan were beside him on the muddy shore of Echo Lake. He shook his head, placed his hands under him, and got to his feet.

Police cars, ambulances, and other emergency vehicles lined Glendale Boulevard. Maria and Morgan got up to stand beside him.

"I don't know how, but it looks like we did it," Bryce

said as he stared back at the small lake. The concrete abutment was damaged now. Bubbles still rose and dispersed around floating pieces of the van's seats on the water's surface.

The surrounding area appeared untouched by the device. An overwhelming feeling of joy consumed him.

"The water seemed to contain it," Morgan said. "Well done, Detective Jacob."

Bryce nodded at the scientist, and then they all started up the embankment. When they neared the road, paramedics ran toward them.

He raised his hands to tell them they were all okay, but the paramedics didn't seem to notice.

Bryce tensed when they were about to collide, but then the man continued running past him. There was an odd *whoosh* feeling as if they'd occupied the same space briefly, but then it was gone.

"What … what was that?" he asked.

Maria stared at him, a hand over her mouth. Morgan had a look of understanding on his face.

Someone called Bryce's name.

When they all turned, Kramer Kay was walking toward them.

"You did it," she shouted at them, tears in her eyes. "I'm so proud of you three."

"Can you tell us what we did and what just happened there?" Bryce asked, feeling disoriented.

"You three saved a lot of lives. That's what happened."

"Okay, but what was that with the paramedic? It was like he didn't see me. But then … he ran *through* me."

"I think they'll explain it better." Kramer pointed behind them.

Bryce spun around.

"Hey, Dad." Lance stood there holding his Frisbee. "Great job, but I'm so happy you're here. I missed you."

Maria gasped beside him as he tried to process what was happening. Maria's husband materialized beside Lance, and then they were hugging. She sputtered his name over and over in his arms.

A moment later, they both disappeared.

"No," Morgan whispered. "No …"

A woman strode up to him.

"It can't be," Morgan said again. "Patricia?"

The woman nodded, holding up her hand. "All intact, my lovely husband. We're home now. You won't believe how wonderful it is over here. Your parents are here, too. Come on, I'll show you how amazing it is."

Morgan glanced once at Bryce. "I can't believe this."

The man seemed consumed with exhilaration, his eyes dancing with joy. He lifted off the pavement and mouthed the words, *thank you* before disappearing from Bryce's sight.

"Come on, Dad," Lance said, holding out his hand. "Let's get you oriented to how it all works over here."

He lifted upward, but before leaving, he spun around to face Kramer.

"It's not every day people are this happy when I've killed them."

Kramer was wiping her eyes with one hand, waving with the other.

He moved farther away, his life review already starting

when he detected Kramer speaking the last words he'd hear her say.

"You're a hero today, Detective Bryce Jacob. Enjoy your real home. Enjoy your son again. May you Rest In Peace. I'm sure we'll bump into each other again …"

Chapter 39

Steven Wallace rolled out of bed. It was four in the morning, and he was awake again. After a few moments, he pushed back the covers and stood from the bed, then walked to the window of his small apartment to look down at the empty street below.

"*Steve?*"

He jumped and spun around. "Who's there?"

"It's Bryce Jacob."

"Where are you?" Wallace leaned against the wall beside the window.

Bryce stepped out of the shadows. "I haven't got a lot of time. It takes massive energy to do this."

"Why are you here?"

"I came to thank you."

Steve scurried back to his bed and sat down as his legs had weakened to where he didn't feel like he could continue standing.

"Thank me?"

"If it weren't for you, I would've never returned to the police station that day. Without your involvement, Cranston would not have gotten to the airport in time, and many people would've died, people who weren't supposed to go yet. You played an important role that day."

"How am I seeing and hearing you? I thought that ability was gone now."

"For the most part, it is, but there was just enough for me to speak with you again. How are you enjoying Cranston's generosity?"

"You know about that?"

"I've been watching."

"After you guys died"—he cleared his throat and looked away briefly—"sorry, touchy subject. Anyway, there was a huge funeral. Cranston said I played a part in stopping the bomb, and many cops donated to help me get my life back on track. No one ever helped me, man. No one. Cranston said he would manage the trust fund to ensure Detective Jacob's friend—that's me—would always be okay. Cool, huh?"

Wallace received no response.

"Jacob, you still there? If you are, I just want to say that I never thought cops would help me in this way—not in a million years. They were always the ones breaking me down, chasing me and beating me. But that changed after you. Now they bring me coffee and dinner and take me to the ball game. I'm like a pal to them. Can you believe it? Even my own dad never did shit like that for me. Course, my dad just beat me all the time …"

Wallace got up from the bed and wandered around the

room.

He was alone.

"Bryce?"

Wallace flicked on the light.

The room was empty.

On his desk in the corner, a pen rolled across the open pad of paper and then stopped at the edge of the desk.

Wallace moved over to the desk and stared down at the pad.

Someone had written something on the paper.

I'm waiting for you, my friend. See you when you get here in a bunch of decades. Life goes on ...

Afterword

Dear Reader,

The first draft of this novel was started in 1999 and was completed in early 2001. This was my first attempt at writing a book that I have ever done. In its first few drafts, it wasn't ready for publication, as I needed to write more and learn more about the writing process as an author. So, while it was going through the editing and rewriting process in 2002, I came up with the idea for Sarah Roberts, a more modern version of Kramer Kay (and Onalee from the short story collection *Twists of Fate (Tale of Hope)*).

This novel became the first I sent query letters to, with publishers in New York and across the United States. There was a glaring error in my query letters that I didn't notice until a year later—and after more than one hundred rejections.

As I mentioned earlier, I needed more experience as a

novelist and hadn't even researched words I thought I knew. In the query letters I sent to literary agents, I wrote "eminent danger" instead of "imminent danger." You'll see in the blurb for this book on Amazon that I used the word imminent. That was intentional—an homage to the mistake from over twenty years ago.

That said, this novel needed even more rewrites and edits and had failed to attract an agent to secure a sale with a reputable publisher.

Side note: this was the novel where I didn't just get form rejections from agencies. I also received several that told me I should stop writing and that I had no career in the publishing business. I imagine they based this on how unprofessional my query letters were. They will remain in the shadows, as I won't mention names here. (I don't recall who most of them were anyway).

Fast-forward to Sarah Roberts's book one, *Dark Visions*, and I'm querying that novel and meeting agents at writers' conferences by 2004.

My journey as an author continued without an agent until I self-published in 2011, then signed with my current agent in 2016; the rest is history.

And now for a few more pieces of nostalgia regarding this novel.

The entire idea for this book came to me from a picture I saw in the newspaper. The photo was taken in a hospital room. Someone appeared to be floating by the window, staring in at the person on the bed. That image made me think the patient in the bed was about to die, and the floating visage was a dead relative coming to greet the liberated soul of the person about to die.

After almost fifteen years of studying and reading about the varieties of religion, philosophy, near-death experiences, and books on death and dying, it was natural for me to move what I had been focusing on into a fictional piece of work.

My search for God and religion, and what comes following death, began after my brother died when I was fourteen. I've spoken briefly about this journey in the Afterwords of other novels, so I'll avoid going into the entire topic here and just say that this novel is dedicated to those who have preceded us in death.

The car that Detective Jacob tells Sergeant Cranston about in that interview room when he's trying to convince him he wasn't crazy was the first car I bought down to every detail. I paid eight hundred bucks in 1985 for a green Buick Century with air conditioning and an 8-track player in the dash. I was able to buy an 8-track-to-cassette converter so I could play cassettes in the car, as 8-tracks were fast becoming a thing of the past in the mid-eighties.

As mentioned a moment ago, this novel is dedicated to those who have gone before us. So, with that in mind, the final three words of this book are my brother's words.

He always used to say, "*Life goes on,*" whenever he'd say goodbye, whether in person or on the phone. Those were the last three words I ever heard him speak in 1983 at Christmas, when we were chatting and wishing each other a Merry Christmas.

Shortly after that Christmas, my brother got a bus in Calgary, Alberta, on January 24, 1984, headed toward Sunshine Mountain Ski Resort, and promptly disappeared—

he was listed as a missing person.

They found his body several weeks later, partially dressed and frozen solid, covered in snow.

"*Life goes on*" is the epitaph on the stone my parents bought for his grave, so I felt those had to be the last three words of this novel.

Just like Bryce, Morgan, and Maria were reunited with their loved ones, I know I'll see him again, as well as my mother, who died in August 2017.

Death isn't the end.

It's the beginning.

And life isn't death.

It's eternal.

God bless you all, and may you live long and prosper. Hug those you love, and embrace your religion, whatever you may believe in.

Have hope in these dark times, and faith.

Love yourself and know that life does go on …

Jonas Saul

About Jonas Saul

Jonas Saul is the bestselling author of the Sarah Roberts Series—more than two million sold!—and has written and published over sixty thrillers. After acquiring an agent, he signed several deals in Hollywood, optioning his Sarah Roberts Series of forty books.

Jonas is regularly invited to be a guest speaker, teacher, or workshop presenter at international writing conferences and film festivals worldwide.

He hosts multiple annual retreats in Greece, where he currently lives—writer's and reader's retreats. He focuses his teaching on how to get tension and emotion in every scene and on every page, how he made it as a creator/writer, the path to success in this business, and the pitfalls to avoid. Visit the Imagine Greece Retreats website at www.imaginegreeceretreats.com, or email him directly to discuss joining a retreat at jonas@imaginegreeceretreats.com.

As an acclaimed author, Jonas is also a professional freelance editor. He lends his editing prowess to several publishers and offers private editing services to clients. His website, www.imaginepress.org, features testimonials from satisfied authors. Jonas is an email away at editor@imaginepress.org for those needing professional editing.

To book Jonas for a speaking engagement at a writer's conference/festival, or to have him on your jury at a film festival, email Jonas directly at jonassaul@icloud.com.

For updates on releases, hit the "Follow" button on Amazon or Bookbub, and join Jonas on Facebook, where he's most active.

Contact Jonas Saul

Linktree: Find me here

Email: jonassaul@icloud.com

Hit the follow buttons here for updates on new releases!

| Amazon Follow | BookBub Follow | Facebook